Jean Jacques Rousseau

AND EDUCATION FROM NATURE

MAXWELL PRESS

Jean Jacques Rousseau
AND EDUCATION FROM NATURE

Gabriel Compayre

Correspondent of the Institute; Director of the Academy of
Lyons; Author of "Psychology Appled to Education," Lectures

on Pedagogy," "A History of Pedagogy," etc.

MAXWELL PRESS

Chennai   New Delhi

MAXWELL PRESS

An Imprint of MJP Publishers

ISBN 978-93-5528-124-1   **MAXWELL PRESS**

No. 44, Nallathambi Street,
Triplicane,
Chennai 600 005

MJP 1405   © Publishers, 2022

Publisher :   **C. Janarthanan**

All rights reserved
Printed and bound in India

This book is a reproduction of an important historical work. Maven Books uses state-of-the-art technology to digitally reconstruct the work, preserving the original format whilst repairing imperfections present in the aged copy. In rare cases, an imperfection in the original, such as a blemish or missing page, may be replicated in our edition. We do, however, repair the vast majority of imperfections successfully; any imperfections that remain are intentionally left to preserve the state of such historical works.

PUBLISHER'S NOTE

The legacy of a country is in its varied cultural heritage, historical literature, developments in the field of economy and science. The top nations in the world are competing in the field of science, economy and literature. This vast legacy has to be conserved and documented so that it can be bestowed to the future generation. The knowledge of this legacy is slowly getting perished in the present generation due to lack of documentation.

Keeping this in mind, the concern with retrospective acquiring of rare books has been accented recently by the burgeoning reprint industry. MAXWELL PRESS is gratified to retrieve the rare collections with a view to bring back those books that were landmarks in their time.

In this effort, a series of rare books would be republished under the banner, "MAXWELL PRESS". The books in the reprint series have been carefully selected for their contemporary usefulness as well as their historical importance within the intellectual. We reconstruct the book with slight enhancements made for better presentation, without affecting the contents of the original edition.

Most of the works selected for republishing covers a huge range of subjects, from history to anthropology. We believe this reprint edition will be a service to the numerous researchers and practitioners active in this fascinating field. We allow readers to experience the wonder of peering into a scholarly work of the highest order and seminal significance.

MAXWELL PRESS

CONTENTS AND SUMMARY

iii

PREFACE

In publishing a series of monographs on the
"Pioneers in Education," those of all nations and
of every age, we have several aims in view.

In the first place, we wish to represent the men
who deserve to have their names on the honour
list in the history of education, all who have in
any remarkable way contributed to the reform
and progress of the instruction and advancement
of humanity; to represent them as they lived; to
show what they thought and did; and to exhibit
their doctrines and methods, and their moral
character.

But after having portrayed each heroic figure
clearly, we must also sketch his background, the
general tendencies of the epoch in which the reformer lived, the scholastic institutions of his country, and the genius, so to speak, of his race, in
order that we may set forth in successive pictures
the struggles and the progress of the civilized races.

In the last place, we wish to do more than write
a historical narrative merely. Our ambition is
higher: it is to bring face to face ideas held long
ago with modern opinions, with the needs and

aspirations of society to-day, and thus to prepare the way for a solution of the pedagogical problems confronting the twentieth century.

If we have chosen J.-J. Rousseau to open this gallery of portraits, it is not because he was a sure guide, an irreproachable leader. But in the cause of education he has been a great inciter of ideas in others, the initiator of the modern movement, the "leader" of most of the educators who came after him. Pestalozzi, Spencer, to cite only two, have undoubtedly been his disciples. He has assailed the routine of tradition; he has broken short off with the past; and if he has not always sown the seed in the field of education, he has at least watered it, rid it of encumbering weeds, leaving to his successors the care of its cultivation and fertilization for later flowering. We therefore render but simple justice and place him where he belongs, when we mention him first.

We dedicate this study and those which follow it to all people who are interested in the cause of education, and who think, as we do, that this question is the vital one, the one upon which depends the future of the people; without which no social reform is possible; that, finally, the progress of education is the question of life and death for society and the individual alike.

ROUSSEAU

I

FOR two centuries the works of J.-J. Rousseau have been read and reread and perpetually annotated. Everything concerning him having been said again and again during this period, pretensions to originality in so minutely explored a subject are scarcely possible. It is, however, always interesting to return to the ideas of an independent and intrepid thinker, one in whose writings paradox and truth are sown broadcast, whose extraordinary influence over the minds of men is a kind of fascination, and of whom M. Melchior de Vogüé could recently say that "he had monopolized our whole political and social future." Rousseau's ideas on education, which also we intend to discuss here, were so original when *Émile* was published in 1762 that they still have claims to novelty, and many a pamphlet, many a book on education, which in 1899 or 1900 earned for its author the reputation of being a daring innovator is, nevertheless, merely the reissue of some of the theories dear to Rousseau. Is it not also true that the light of progress and the broader horizons revealed by the succession of the ages are able to rejuvenate and reillumine a subject to all appearance exhausted?

Émile is a knotty, tangled book, full of matter, and to such an extent is the true mingled with the false, imagination and hazardous dream with keen, accurate observation and reasoning power, that at first a full comprehension of it is impossible. It is not one of those simple, straightforward works which yield their secret from the outset; it is an intricate composition, half novel, half philosophical treatise, which — supposing that Rousseau had not written *La Nouvelle Héloïse* — would be sufficient to justify the title of a recent study by M. Faguet, *J.-J. Rousseau, romancier français,* just as it gave him the right to be called "a psychologist of the first degree," an appellation bestowed on him by Mr. Davidson, an American author. The propositions advanced in it by Rousseau, with all the ardor of his fervid imagination and all the allurements of an enchanted pen, are at first disconcerting to the reader: some minds are captivated, others roused to distrust. Many are the perusals necessary before a path can be traced through this confusion of philosophic meditation and sentimental fancy. Did not his own steps wander, as when, for example, having introduced Émile to us as an orphan, he makes him the recipient of letters from his father and mother as a means of inducing him to learn to read?

Though at first one is tempted to protest against the audacities and blunders of a venturesome mind lacking in balance, yet, on reflection, it becomes apparent that the greater part of his paradoxes conceal a fund of truth — not, indeed, a commonplace, but an original conception, a thought reaching into the future, the accuracy of which will, little by little, be proved by experience. Oftentimes the myths with which he seemed most infatuated receive from himself a decisive reply. Elsewhere, to find oneself in agreement with him, it is only necessary to set aside the tricks of style with which he chose to envelop his ideas. In short, *Émile* is a combative book "full of fire and smoke," and as on a battlefield a just idea of the positions which have been carried can only be obtained after the smoke of the cannonade has cleared away, so, to grasp and distinguish the results of Rousseau's rapid advance on the field of the new education, the sound of the sonorous sentences, the tumult of the figures of speech, apostrophe, and prosopopæia in his inflamed harangues must be allowed to die away. Unquestionably, certain portions of *Émile* have grown old, but others have required the passage of a hundred years and more ere they could be truly understood and could present themselves in their full force.

The preceding sentences describe the spirit in which this study has been conceived: less to criticise Rousseau than to bring to light the treasures of abiding truth which he has, as it were, buried in a book described truly by him as "the most useful and considerable" of his writings. It were an easy matter to convict him of flagrant utopianism: this commonplace task of refutation will occupy us no more than is absolutely necessary. Without concealing any of the sophisms of *Émile*, our principal aim will be to ascertain in what Rousseau's guidance may still be useful to us. True criticism is that which insists upon the good, and deals with the bad only to explain it. Rather for posterity and for the future did Rousseau speak than for his contemporaries and the period in which he lived. In the forgotten recesses of *Émile* lurk more than one reflection which, hitherto unperceived, proves to be fruitful in instruction for the people of our time, and directly suited to present requirements; so great was the perspicacity of a philosopher, a "finder of hidden springs," who, thirty years in advance, had predicted the French Revolution at the same time that he was preparing it. Far greater in importance, however, than a multitude of isolated truths, is the general spirit animating the entire book. *Émile* deserves to remain the eternal object of the educator's meditation, were it only because it is an act of faith and trust in humanity.

II

Rousseau is truly an initiator; nay more, a revolutionary. He forestalled the generations of 1789, even those of 1793, which claimed to be the reconstitutors of society and the regenerators of the human race, as expressed in Barère's energetic speech to his colleagues of the Convention, "You are convoked for the recommencement of history." In such times of crisis and disturbance the attention of vigilant thinkers is naturally directed to children and education; for by education alone can one expect to guide new souls along the paths of a regenerated existence. Such was Rousseau's ambition. He was the reformer, the dreamer, if you will, who, in his ardent protest against realities which he condemns, aspires in all things to a radical renovation of human institutions. This appeal to the ideal — to leave unmentioned those first attempts by which he had already trained his critical enthusiasm — had as its result the splendid trilogy of his principal works, published in quick succession in three years, *La Nouvelle Héloïse*, in 1759, the *Contrat social* and

Émile in a single year, 1762; three masterpieces which, despite diversity of form and subject, proceed from a common inspiration, tending equally, as they do, to the reformation of society, the first in its domestic morals, the second in its political constitution, and lastly *Émile*, in the laws of education for children and youths.

Powerful as may be Rousseau's inventive originality, we are far from claiming that his educational system, which for eight years occupied his meditations, is a stroke of genius, a miraculous revelation, neither prepared nor announced by anything in the past. Rousseau had his forerunners and inspirers. A Benedictine — Dom Cajot — who might have employed his time to better purpose, wrote a large volume on *Rousseau's Plagiarisms:* the plagiarisms we deny, but imitation and indebtedness must be admitted. The glory of even the most original geniuses suffers no diminution though it be established that some of their most famous conceptions were dimly perceived and outlined before they succeeded, as it were, in giving substance to vague intellectual shadow by the intensity of their personal reflection. Rousseau was impregnated with Montaigne and quotes him constantly. He had read and "devoured" the Port Royal books. Fénelon, "wise" Locke, "good" Rollin, and "learned" Fleury dictated

some of his finest precepts.   Locke, with his practical
mind and somewhat prosy sound sense, doubtless
has no great resemblance to Rousseau; he inspired
him, nevertheless, in his campaign against weak,
effeminate education, and also against "bookish"
instruction.   Rousseau does not appear to have been
familiar with Rabelais, yet there are obvious simi-
larities between Émile's education and that which
Épistémon instituted for the profit of young Gargantua, that other imaginary being and pupil of
nature.   Not only did Rousseau study and annotate
the *Projet de paix perpétuelle* by the abbé of Saint-
Pierre, that man so fertile in projects, he continues
it by his utilitarian tendencies and taste for ethical
education.   Other names might well be mentioned.
. . . But the author of *Émile* transfigures what-
ever he touches, and transforms all that he borrows.
His exuberant imagination gives fresh form and
color to ideas lent by others: timid, they become
imperious; vague, they obtain a sharp definition;
like feeble shrubs, which, transplanted to a rich and
fertile soil, grow up into vigorous trees.

Of all Rousseau's predecessors it is perhaps Turgot
who most clearly traced out the new paths.   The
author of *Émile* does not appear, indeed, to have had
any knowledge of the views which Turgot expounded
in the long epistle,—a veritable memoir,—which he

addressed in 1751 to Mme. de Graffigny, the then celebrated authoress of *Lettres péruviennes*. It is not a rare thing, however, for minds in motion to meet at the same period of time in the same inspirations without mutual arrangement. Earlier than Rousseau by ten years, and with equal conviction, Turgot preached the return to nature. "Our education," said he, "is mere pedantry: everything is taught us quite against nature."— "Nature must be studied and consulted, so that she may be assisted and we be saved the detriment of thwarting her." — "Children's heads are filled with a mass of abstract notions which they cannot grasp, and all the time nature is calling them to her through every perceptible object." Down to the fundamental maxim of *Émile* on the original innocence of our inclinations, everything has already been admitted by Turgot: "All the virtues have been sown by nature in the heart of man: the one thing needful is to let them blossom forth."

The examples quoted are sufficient to make it apparent that ideas in germ were diffused in the atmosphere around Rousseau and that he collected them for development. It is, however, no less apparent that from himself, from his own rich store and *à priori* views of human nature, if not from a practical experience which he lacked, was drawn the substance of his treatise *De l'Éducation*. Rousseau reasoned and imagined still more than he beheld and observed. This is not because he overlooked the necessity for observation: he was fully alive to it and knew exactly in what he was deficient to treat with competence the great subject upon which he was entering. This is proved by the letter written by him to one of his protectresses, Mme. de Créquy, on the 15th of January, 1759, when, *La Nouvelle Héloïse* being finished, he had begun in earnest the composition of *Émile:* "Speaking of education, there are some ideas on this subject which I should be tempted to put on paper if I had a little assistance; but some observations which I cannot supply are necessary. You, Madam, are a mother and, though devout, a philosopher; you have educated your son. Were you willing, in your spare moments, to jot down some reflections on this matter and communicate them to me, you would be well repaid for your trouble should they assist me in the production of a useful work." The unnatural father who had not reared his own offspring was reduced to begging the experience of others. . . .

Rousseau was aware, then, that a study of childhood is necessary before rules for the management of children can be established. If it is correct to say that he endowed France with a new literature and that he was one of the ancestors of romanticism, it is equally correct to affirm that in his manner he inaugurated those important studies which for some years have been in vogue under the name of "psychology of the child." A well-stocked chapter on this new psychology could easily be made by collecting the numerous accurate, subtle observations on the character and tastes of infancy which are scattered through the long pages of *Émile.* "Children always think only of the present. . . . I know of nothing for which, with a little ingenuity, one cannot inspire them with a taste, a passion even, and this without rendering them vain or jealous of the acquirements of others. Their vivacity, their imitative mind, and especially their natural gayety are sufficient for this. . . . Every age in life, and especially the age of infancy, desires to create, to imitate, to produce, to manifest power and activity."

These quotations might be multiplied many times, and it might be shown how greatly Rousseau delighted in studying children — alas! why must it be added, other people's children? It is sad to see him take up his position at the window of his dreary house, empty through his own fault, to watch the children coming out of school and to observe by stealth the conversations, games, and childish actions of the little scholars. . . . "Never did a man," says he in the last but one of the *Rêveries d'un promeneur solitaire*, "find more pleasure than myself in watching youngsters romp and play together!" And he adds, "If I have made some progress in the knowledge of the human heart, it is the pleasure that I used to take in watching and observing children which has earned me that knowledge."

How much more accurate would Rousseau's psychology have been, however, if, instead of a fleeting attention paid to a few street Arabs, whom he watched for a moment at their frolics, he had been able to exercise the attentive observation of a father who, day by day, watches the birth and development of his son's mind.

It is, moreover, noteworthy that the solicitude for education came to Rousseau because he had criminally abandoned his five children, as though he had felt himself compelled to make partial reparation for the most serious of all his moral shortcomings. "The ideas with which my fault has filled my mind have contributed to turn my meditations to the subject of education. . . ."

Rousseau was also deficient in professional experience of instruction. I am well aware that to the long list of occupations which he took up in the course of his vagrant youth and Bohemian existence, when he was successively engraver's apprentice, recorder's clerk, clerk, secretary, music copyist, — Grimm, who did not like him, once advised him to sell lemonade, — the occupation of tutor must be added; but he practised it so little and so ill! . . . In 1739 — he was then twenty-seven — Bonnot de Mably, royal provost at Lyons, confided to him the education of his two sons. At first he applied himself to this task, thinking himself fitted for it. He was soon disabused, however: "I did nothing worth doing." He could only employ three methods of discipline, "always useless and pernicious with children," — sentiment, argument, and anger. Sentiment he never renounces, as, when reproving Émile for a fault, the tutor will only say, "My boy, you have hurt me!" . . . Argument, however, he excludes pitilessly from the child's instruction, convinced henceforth, contrary to Locke's doctrine, that it is not advisable to argue and reason too early with children, "who, though they may be reasoners, are no more reasonable for that." Quickly finding distasteful a profession for which he was in no way suited, Rousseau resigned it at the end of a year, but not before he had drawn up for M. de Sainte-Marie, one of his two pupils, an educational scheme in which neither thought nor style announce the brilliant and profound author of *Émile*.

If Rousseau was neither an assiduous observer of

childhood **nor** a professor — nor even a pupil; as he never studied in a connected manner, and was a student only of what has been called "the University of Charmettes"; as a compensation he felt much and lived much; and for the formation of a powerful mind, a regular course of study at Plessis College would certainly have been less advantageous and efficacious than that agitated existence which led Rousseau into all grades of society, into drawing-room and anteroom, which made him in succession the friend of philosophers and the table companion of great lords, a plebeian on good terms with the people, and the petted favorite of great ladies, countesses, duchesses, and marchionesses.

It is indisputable that Rousseau put much of his personality, that he worked many reminiscences of his life and reflections of his mind, into the conception of the model pupil which he fashioned for humanity. Montaigne said, "I am the substance of my book." Is this so with Rousseau? Could he also say, as Amiel insinuates, "My system and myself make one"? Did he conceive Émile in his likeness and in his resemblance? Amiel claims that he weaves nothing but his own substance into his most magnificent theories, that he is first and foremost a "subjective." We do not deny this, and we are aware that as a general rule educators have a natural tendency to project themselves, as it were, into the plans which they recommend for others' imitation.   When Rousseau, for example, suppresses all didactic teaching in instruction, what does he do beyond setting up as a rule his own experience?   "What little I know, I learned by myself.   I could never learn anything from a master. . . ."   Rousseau is self-taught, and so is Émile.

On the other hand, however, on how many other points are the fancies of Émile's education in formal opposition with the realities of Rousseau's existence? It follows naturally that people satisfied with their destiny recommend to others what they have found to answer in their own case.   But Rousseau was dissatisfied with himself and his lot, no less than with society.   The education which he desired, appears, as a consequence, to have been conceived in an effort of reaction against his own condition, as a contrast to the imprudences from which he had suffered, and the errors or faults committed by him.   Poor stricken mind and infirm, diseased body, he consoles himself by evoking the ideal image of a hardy child, healthy in mind and body.   He requites himself for his wretchedness and imperfections by creating a happy, perfect being.

He says, for example: "As yet I had conceived

nothing. I had felt everything." Is it not so as to escape the consequences of this precocious stimulation, which had made him morbidly sensitive, and demoralized for life, that, going to the opposite extreme, he leaves Émile unacquainted with all sentimental emotion until he is fifteen? He read to excess; before he was ten years old he had devoured a whole library of novels. Is it because of this that, detesting and anathematizing books, he forbids them absolutely to Émile? I do not know, said M. Brunetière, one of our great writers whose childhood and youth were to such a degree lacking in guidance. He cannot, indeed, be said to have had a family: his mother died in giving birth to him; his father, after having spoiled him, deserted him. Nobody brought him up. . . . How, after that, could the temptation be avoided of imagining a situation quite the reverse, by which Émile is given a tutor who does not lose sight of him for a second, a mentor who will accompany and protect him in his every action right up to the threshold of the nuptial chamber?

In evil surroundings, compromised by humiliating society, Rousseau was conscious of all the dignity and nobility of mind that he had lost in the contaminations of his existence: then, to educate a man in honor and virtue, let us eliminate all exterior circumstances which may sully and degrade him.   Émile shall live alone, far from mankind. . . . Rousseau lounged in servants' hall and antechamber; he took part in the distractions of fashionable life; he frequented the drawing-rooms of Paris, and now and again allowed himself to be seduced by society's artifices;   he contracted numerous frivolous love intrigues.   None of these things for the ideal man: the country, fresh air, outdoor life with its simplicity, a pure love, single and deep, nothing but nature. . . . "Farewell, Paris, city of noise, smoke, and mud, where woman no longer believes in purity nor man in virtue!   Farewell, Paris, our quest is love, happiness, and innocence; never shall we be sufficiently remote from thee! . . ."

Much of *Émile* is, then, a visionary structure erected expressly to make a contrast to Rousseau's actual life.   To excuse, or at least explain, the generation of all the wild delusions of *Émile*, let us never lose sight of the inward struggle which took place in its author's heart between what was noble in his aspirations and base in his existence: the striking incongruity between the adoration which he professed for the ideal and the pitiful reality of the circumstances in which he was placed and for which he was in part responsible.   This man, of whom Grimm said that "he had nearly always been miserable," bruised by the strangest adventures, weighed down by physical sickness, and who felt that he was dying whilst engaged in composing *Émile;* still more disturbed by imaginary ills which an anxious mind invented for him; embittered by that kind of mania of persecution which from year to year was to increase and was finally to drive him to suicide; exasperated against a state of society with whose vices he was the better acquainted through having participated in them; humiliated by the remembrance of what he called his youthful "rascalities"; ashamed later of his cohabitation with an inn servant whose vulgarity must more than once have been a heavy burden to him: he felt the need of throwing himself back upon an ideal world, there to seek a fleeting forgetfulness of his moral infirmities, a compensation for his misfortunes, in revenge for the frailties of his character and the gloom of his destiny. If his life was often a painful drama, certain parts of *Émile* shall be idyls and pastorals of real poetic charm. He has said so: "The impossibility of attaining to actual beings has cast me into the land of delusions: I have made myself societies of perfect creatures. . . ." The exaggerations and phantasies to which we shall have to direct attention in *Émile* will often only be deliberate inventions which did not at all delude their inventor. As he put it when writing in 1763 to the prince of Wirtemberg concerning the scheme of education which he had addressed to him for his daughter Sophie, brought up in conformity with the principles of *Émile:* "These are, perhaps, only the hallucinations of a delirious man. . . . The comparison of what is with what should be has given me a romantic mind, and has always driven me far from what goes on."

What Rousseau would fain have been and was not, Émile is to be, or at least that is Rousseau's desire.

III

"Pardon me my paradoxes, ordinary reader," exclaims Rousseau somewhere. The best way of pardoning them is to attempt to extract the core of truth which they contain. Once we have deprived the essential principles of his system of the violent form in which this conjurer of thought was pleased to envelop them, it remains for us to gather together the general rules, the characteristic positive and unquestioned truths in *Émile* which modern education will never relinquish.

"Man is born free and everywhere he is fettered," thus begins *Contrat social.*

"Man is born good and everywhere he has become corrupt," such is the sense of the preamble to *Émile.*

Rousseau delights in these absolute statements: he likes concise, peremptory formulas which compel attention.

To his political sophism, "The universal will of the people is always right," corresponds his psychological sophism, "Nature is fundamentally good."

Such is the initial error which gives rise to all that is false in *Émile*. The bitterest and most incisive of pessimists when judging actual society, Rousseau is the most indulgent of optimists when he considers, beyond the work of man, the work of Providence, that is to say, nature.

Nature is good and beneficent. Her creatures are pure, so long as they have not been perverted, corrupted, disfigured, and sophisticated by a pretended civilization which is merely a long decadence. On this point, Rousseau was in agreement with a number of his contemporaries. D'Holbach said, "Man is vicious because he has been made so"; and Diderot, "A natural man used to exist; into this natural man an artificial man has been introduced." Rousseau comes back insistently to the same doctrine. "Let us lay down as an incontestable maxim that the first movements of nature are always right, and that there is no original perversity in man's heart. . . . All characters are good and healthy in themselves. . . . There is no error in nature. . . ."

Doubtless it would be within one's right to stop Rousseau at once and ask him to explain this flagrant contradiction: man is naturally good, and society, man's work, is bad. . . . But he is not disturbed by this incongruity. Faithful to the opinion which he had expressed in the two *Discours* which began his reputation, he clings tenaciously to his utopia. He repeats in every form that, with its customs and prejudices, society is detestable and perverted, that it must be thoroughly reformed. Let us revive nature's authority and substitute it for the rule of ancient and antiquated tradition; let us supersede the empire of stern discipline and oppressive restriction, which mutilate and deform the human faculties, by the reign of young liberty, which will assist in their expansion.

By such a challenge hurled at every human institution, Rousseau had in view more than a simple pedagogical reformation: he was announcing a social revolution. Authentically he is the father of the revolutionists whose idol he was to become: let us not forget that Marat, in 1788, read *Contrat social* to the cheers of an enthusiastic audience.

From the educational point of view, the principle laid down by Rousseau has for consequence the necessity of reconstructing natural man, "original" man according to the expression of which he had already made use in his *Discours sur l'inégalité parmi les hommes*, man as he was in the primitive scheme of nature and Providence — for in Rousseau's religious mind, behind nature is Providence, who is the keystone of his philosophical doctrine — man, in short, as he would be, if social life and its long corruption had not perverted him, natural man, in a word, and not "human man."

Let us not stop to demonstrate that Rousseau is in error, that there are in nature germs for evil as well as good, and that education is consequently something more than a complaisant auxiliary, that it should be a resistive force which corrects and compensates. Let us rather bear in mind that the contrary opinion, which also was absolute, that of a nature essentially bad, vitiated in its origin, and pre-destined exclusively to evil had long prevailed and still held sovereign sway. And from this radical condemnation of humanity proceeded a strict and rigid education, made up chiefly of repression, bristling with prohibition and chastisement, which conceded nothing to the child's native liberty. Trial had been made of all disciplinary instruments save one, precisely the one which alone could succeed, — well regulated liberty. Rousseau arises, and with *éclat* he opposes the conception of the old fallen Adam whose fated inheritance must be eradicated from every man by the contrary doctrine of a humanity instinctively impelled to good and, accordingly, destined to develop in full liberty. The contradictory movements of the ideas which appear in succession on the theatre of human opinion recall in some degree those comedies in which a speaker primed with one side of a question is answered by another, who goes to the opposite extreme, the better to display the conflict of sentiments. Both the one and the other are wrong, but the collision of opposite opinions will cause the truth which lies between to stand out. Even at the risk of straining his voice and exaggerating his repartee, it was good that an eloquent thinker, in reply to those who for two thousand years had repeated the lament of degenerate mankind, should testify to his confidence and happy faith in the natural powers and tendencies of man: thus, thirty years before the French Revolution promulgated the *Déclaration des droits de l'homme*, a pedagogue announced the declaration of childhood's rights, of its right to an education of liberty. "It is wrong," says Rousseau, "always to speak to children of their duties, never of their rights." *Émile* was, as it were, the charter of childhood's freedom.

Paradox begets paradox, and from the erroneous principle which serves as the starting-point of *Émile* has sprung the entire series of pedagogical falsities, for which Rousseau has been so severely but so justly reproved, what Nisard called his "enormities," and the English pedagogue, R. Hébert Quick, "his extravagances."

The first of these capital errors is that education, at any rate to the age of twelve, should be strictly "negative." "Positive" education will only begin for Émile after a long intellectual idleness and an equally lengthy moral inaction. Since nature tends of itself towards its ends, she should be left alone. In *La Nouvelle Héloïse,* Julie was already of opinion that education consists "in doing nothing at all." The best educator is the one who acts least, intervening only to remove obstacles which would hinder the free play of nature, or to create circumstances favorable to it.

Education is to be doubly negative: in discipline and instruction alike. On the one hand, no commands are to be given to the child; on the other, he is to be taught nothing.

Hence, no moral authority, no material discipline in the child's upbringing. Neither precepts nor chastisements, at least such as are inflicted by human intention, nor rewards of any kind. No punishments other than those which are the natural results of the action and the consequences of the fault committed. It is the principle which we find again in Herbert Spencer, "Never offer to the indiscreet desires of a child any other obstacles than physical ones." The hand of man is to be nowhere apparent. Émile must remain alone in the presence of nature and her might. Knowledge of good and evil is not for children. . . . The inspiration of this kind of disciplinary nihilism was perhaps obtained by Rousseau from his personal remembrances. "He had never obeyed," says Amiel. "He had known neither kindly family control nor firm scholastic discipline." Émile does not know what obedience is, nor disobedience either, as he never receives commands. He has no idea that a human will other than his own can exist. He is subjected to one law only, an inflexible one, however, that of the possible and the impossible. He knows no other authority than that of nature's laws, no other dependence than that of the imperative necessity of things.

Would it serve any useful purpose to reply to Rousseau, to point out to him that he is in error, that there is indeed nothing more artificial and contrary to nature than this so-called natural education, in which is suppressed the most natural thing in the world, — the authority of parents and masters? What? No longer could anything be expected in the direction of a child's conduct from either the tender insinuations of a mother's affection, or the injunctions of a father's strong will, at once gentle and firm, or the persuasive exhortations of a kindly and watchful master? It may be wise to exclude from discipline the caprices of maladroit parents who command and countermand, who go from the extreme of blind complacency to that of brutal severity; but what folly it would be to reject the benefits to the moral education of a child permitted by the action of authority exercised with prudence and wisdom. Prevent the birth of vice, and you will have done enough for virtue, protests Rousseau. Just as he says a little later, Prevent error and prejudice from obtaining entrance into Émile's mind, and you will have done enough for knowledge. No, prevention of evil is not sufficient: it is necessary to teach good. If Émile's intellect lies fallow for twelve years, it will be like those fields which the husbandman does not till or sow: weeds will spring up in alarming abundance; and when their destruction is desired, it will be too late. Rousseau was better inspired in *La Nouvelle Héloïse*, in which he said: "A good nature should be cultivated. . . . Children must be taught to obey their mother."

In the study which he has devoted to *Émile*, and which is the best we know, John Morley remarks with reason that omission of the principle of authority is the fundamental weakness of Rousseau's system. In this system, says he, in effect, the child is always to suppose that it is following its own judgment or impulses. . . . It must not feel the constraint of a will other than its own. The parent and the master must not intervene; . . . as though parents were not a part of nature? . . . And, moreover, why are the effects of conduct upon the actor's own physical well-being to be the only effects honored with the title of being natural, neglecting the feelings of approbation or disapproval which this same conduct inspires? One of the most important of educating influences is lost if the young are not taught to place the feelings of others in a front place. The acquirement of many excellent qualities is threatened if a child, in its ignorance and frailty, is not inclined naturally to respect, in its parents and masters, a better-informed authority and an experience riper than its own.

No less serious is the error in respect of the other aspect of negative education, — the adjournment of instruction. Here Rousseau becomes enthusiastic, and he impressively eulogizes the supposed benefits of the long mental idleness which he imposes on his pupil. "May I venture to state the greatest, the most important, the most useful rule in all education? it is, not to gain time, but to lose it. . . . Reading is the scourge of childhood. . . . Apparent facility in learning is the ruin of children. . . . I teach the art of being ignorant. . . ." No books, then, no verbal lesson. Émile will grow up like a little savage, without intellectual culture, exercising only his body and his senses. The ideal is for him to remain ignorant as long as possible, to reach the age of twelve not even knowing "how to distinguish his right hand from his left." Rousseau, who goes into ecstasies in face of his work, says, with humorous exaggeration, "I would as soon require a child of ten to be five feet tall as to be judicious;" . . . and again, "Émile would not hesitate to give the whole Académie des sciences" — supposing that he is aware of its existence — "for a pastry-cook's shop."

Undoubtedly, not everything is blameworthy in the inactive, expectant education which Rousseau recommends. Let us retain this much of it, that it is well not to be in haste, not to outdistance the progress natural to the age; that it is imprudent and dangerous to weary a child with a precocious and premature education; that one risks exhausting its powers by fatiguing them too soon. But what a number of arguments array themselves against the system which, by a contrary abuse, leaves the intellectual faculties uncultured during the first twelve years, perhaps the most fruitful of one's whole life! Rousseau himself points out an objection that might well be final: it is that the mind, so long enervated by inaction, will become incapable of action, and "will be absorbed by matter." How can it be hoped that Émile, who has studied nothing, will all at once have the desire and ability to learn everything, that his dormant thought will spring into wakefulness at the magic summons of his tutor, to acquire as by enchantment all the attainments in which he is deficient? And especially, how can the versatility and flexibility of the intellectual organs required by every study be assured him in a short time, when their preparation by continued exercise and slow initiation has been neglected?   Finally, if Rousseau's statement were true, if the child were incapable of all abstract study, if it were necessary to prohibit all mental work for it till the age of twelve, can the result be imagined? It would be necessary to close all elementary schools, and the instruction of the people would be impossible.

I am well aware that Rousseau, as a substitute for books and formal lessons, appeals to nature's teachings. Émile has learned nothing by heart; he scarcely knows what a book is. To make up for this, he knows much from experience; "he reads in nature's book." First, let us point out that nature does not consent to play the part of schoolmistress, with which Rousseau wishes to saddle her, to such an extent. The proof of this is that he is himself forced to resort to artifices, to the most complicated stratagems, to inculcate into his pupil the rare gleams of knowledge which lighten the darkness of his ignorance. Nature needs a stage carpenter to prepare the laboriously arranged scenes in which an attempt is made to provide Émile with an equivalent for the lessons of everyday education. Such is the juggler episode, intended to reveal to him some notions of elementary physics; such is the conversation with Robert the gardener on the origin of property. Doubtless, Émile will know more thoroughly the few little things thus learned by himself. But not only will his instruction be singularly limited, this teaching from experience and nature will also be very slow. It will take him months and years to discover what he might just as well have learned in a few hours, by means of well-arranged lessons or well-chosen reading. Is, then, everything that the clear diction of a professor can put within the reach of the smallest scholar, all the light that books can bring to the dawning intelligence, to be useless? And is it to benefit Émile nothing that he is heir to a long line of generations who have worked, thought, and written, although that effort of centuries has accumulated treasuries of truths upon which newcomers need only draw in order to derive instruction?

It is sufficient, moreover, to condemn a system which would result in nothing less than the suppression of all moral discipline and all didactic teaching during the first period of life, that Rousseau, to apply it, is obliged to place his pupil in an abnormal situation, to set him free from the ordinary conditions of existence, to isolate him in a kind of exile, to withdraw him from his parents' control in order to confide him to a stranger's keeping.   Astonishment has been expressed that Rousseau, a sincere friend and an apostle of family life,—we shall soon be convinced of that,—suppressed parents, brothers, and sisters in his educational novel.   Where are the exquisite pictures which he had outlined in *La Nouvelle Héloïse* of the games and education mutually shared by Julie's children brought up under their mother's eyes?   If Rousseau is recanting, it is because he was forced into doing so by the necessity of giving an appearance of practical achievement to his dream of negative education.   How, indeed, can one suppose that a father and mother are capable of holding sufficiently aloof from the education of a son reared by themselves, to keep from influencing him by admonitions, severe at need, or by affectionate caresses?   It was absolutely necessary that the hero of natural education should live alone in his childhood, without either parents, comrades, God, or master, — for God is not mentioned to him till much later, when he is eighteen; and as for the tutor who bears him company he is, properly speaking, neither master nor professor: he is simply a guardian, a vigilant sentinel, whose orders are to protect Émile against influences from without, against everything which could hinder nature's beneficent action, and whose part is restricted to forming around his pupil, as it were, an isolating wall.

This strange isolation of a child to whom all intercourse with the rest of the human species is forbidden is, then, only a fanciful fabrication which Rousseau required in order to throw into clear relief the novelties of his plan. We see little more in it than a trick of composition, and it would consequently be superfluous to indulge in irony against a fiction which the author disavows in many passages of his book; a fiction the absurd improbability of which is sufficient to demonstrate that he never thought of making it the universal rule of education. "I point out the goal to make for: I do not say that it can be reached." How suppose that Rousseau seriously thought it possible to realize a system the least defect of which would be that it suppress every other function than the tutor's, since half mankind would be kept employed as educators for twenty years, and as Mme. de Staël said, "Grandfathers at most would be free to begin a personal career"? A mentor, indeed, would have to be found for every Telemachus; that is, for every child to be educated. The Christian faith, in its fervors, inspired the "stylites," those extravagant anchorites who passed their lives on the summit of a column, 'twixt earth and sky, as though it were desired in this way to present in a striking and absurd form the necessity of rupture with the world. Similarly, Rousseau's naturalistic faith suggested to him the invention of an exceptional being who is to live and grow up far from society, by a sort of hypothesis whose object is to make the power of nature's education evident. It is unthinkable that Rousseau should so imperiously call upon a mother to suckle her child, only to carry it away from her tenderness and remove it from her care as soon as it is weaned. No, he merely wished, in an artificial framework, to give free rein to his visions. Émile is no real being: he is a creature of reason, as it were, an engine of war invented to combat society.

At bottom, as will be seen by reference to other passages of *Émile* and to Rousseau's other writings, domestic education never had a more fervent partisan.

Often in his *Correspondence* does he return to the praise of family life. It is true that in his *Considérations sur le gouvernement de Pologne*, dating from 1772, he has altered his opinion and, by a fresh contradiction, declares himself ardently for a third solution, education in common. Rousseau is a man of successive impulses, each in turn defended with the same impetuosity. To the Poles he resolutely advises national education pushed to its last extreme, the teachings of the *Republic* of Plato, which absorbs the man into the citizen, and confiscates the individual to hand him bodily to the State. Rousseau was divided all his life between the doctrine of individualism and that of socialism, between State sovereignty and man's liberty.

He says: "The good social institutions are those which can best change man's nature, remove his absolute existence to replace it by a quite relative one. . . . It is by public education that minds are given a national form. . . . Public education, on lines prescribed by the government, is one of the fundamental maxims of all popular government. . . ." And again, in the *Encyclopædia* article on *Political Economy*, "As each man's reason is not left sole arbiter of his duties, so much the less should children's education be left to the opinions and prejudices of fathers. . . ."

This is far removed from Émile's individualistic education, and we willingly admit that it is impossible to push unconscious freedom in the mutability of conflicting opinions and impetuous contradictions farther than Rousseau does. And yet, in spite of all, we maintain that, viewing his aspirations as a whole, Rousseau is in favor of domestic education. Let us first read that fine page of *Émile*, in which he claims that a girl should be brought up by her mother, and vigorously refutes the chimeras of platonic education. He protests "against that civil promiscuity which mixes both sexes in the same employments, in the same labors, and which cannot but give rise to the most intolerable abuses,—against that subversion of the gentlest sentiments of nature sacrificed to an artificial sentiment which owes its existence to them, — as though it were not necessary to have a natural hold to form conventional ties; as though love of kindred were not the principle of that which is due to the State; as though it were not through the little fatherland, which is the family, that the heart is attached to the larger one; as though it were not the good son, the good father, and the good husband, who make the good citizens. . . ."

At the great word "family" Rousseau's imagination takes fire, so much 'the more, perhaps, as he himself neither knew its joys nor performed its obligations. Talk not to him either of colleges for boys or of convents for girls! Colleges he dismisses in a word as "laughable establishments," — and it is because he had spoken of them in this disdainful way that he thought, according to what he recounts in the *Confessions*, that he had drawn upon himself the hatred of the Jesuits, of whom, from prudence, he had made it a rule "never to speak, either well or ill." As for convents, because they do not exist in Protestant nations, he considered the latter superior to Catholic nations.

In *La Nouvelle Héloïse*, Rousseau sharply reprimands parents who put their children into the hands of strange masters, "as though a tutor could replace a father. . . ." Elsewhere, in his letters to the prince of Würtemberg, he writes: "There is no paternal eye but a father's, and no maternal eye but a mother's. I should like to devote twenty reams of paper to repeating those two lines to you, so much am I convinced that everything depends on them. . . ."

Besides this, it is known with what eloquence, in *Émile* itself, Rousseau recalled mothers to their duty, as far as nursing is concerned. Undoubtedly he is not the first who did so. In Rome itself, in the second century, the philosopher Favorinus said, "Is it not being only half a mother to confide one's children to paid nurses? . . ." Words of kindness, in agreeable contrast with the harsh manners and severity of a society, one of whose most illustrious representatives, Cicero, wrote a century earlier, in his *Tusculanes,* "When a child dies young, consolation is easily found; when it dies in the cradle, it is not even a matter for concern. . . ."

In the years which preceded the publication of *Émile,* doctors and moralists had undertaken the same campaign, but they had carried it on without vigor. Rousseau put his whole heart into it, and as Mme. de Genlis said, "Wisdom is less persuasive than enthusiasm. Rousseau repeated what others had said; but he did not advise: he commanded and was obeyed."

In bringing the mothers back to the cradles, Rousseau was not solely concerned with the child's interest and its physical needs. "If he demanded the nurse's milk, it was to have the mother's affection."

In his eyes, the child is, as it were, the bearer of the family virtues, the pledge and at the same time the guarantee of conjugal love. It is the sacred bond which indissolubly unites husband and wife. It is the child which sustains and rekindles the domestic hearth, by the joy which its winning presence brings to it, as by the common duties which its education imposes. In the appeal which Rousseau addresses to parents, the father is no more forgotten than the mother. After saying: "Would you recall every one to his highest duties? Begin with the mothers," he adds: "As the mother is the true nurse, the father is the true teacher. . . . The father will make excuses: business, he will say, duties. . . . Doubtless, the least important is to be a father! . . ."

But let us return to Rousseau's chimeras, to what he himself described in his *Préface* as the "dreams of a visionary," without giving up the idea of seeking and finding in them some grains of truth. To the illusion of negative education is attached that of "successive" education. Here Rousseau is going to contradict his essential principle, which is to follow nature. If there be, indeed, a fixed law of nature, it is that she creates nothing abruptly, but always proceeds by slow, imperceptible evolution. "With her," says Mme. Necker de Saussure, "one can nowhere lay hold on a beginning; she is not to be surprised in the act of creation, and it seems that she is forever developing." From this very accurate conception has issued the fine system of "progressive education." But Rousseau imagined another thing: a fragmentary, seriate education, divided into three periods. He forgets that nature makes the several functions of a human creature advance abreast in their development, and that education should accordingly conform to this simultaneous evolution of the various bodily and mental faculties. Quite otherwise, he shatters the true unity of the human being. "It is," says Mme. d'Épinay, "as though children were forbidden to move their arms and use their hands whilst learning to walk." In the first place, by an absolute dualism, Rousseau disassociates the mind from the body. "Nature intended the body to develop before the mind." But of the mind itself, instead of one, he makes three. In the artificial story of Émile, there are three phases, radically distinct and separate from each other. Until twelve years old, physical life and sense exercise: nothing for either intelligence or heart. Émile, at the age of twelve, is only a hardy animal, an agile "roebuck." From twelve to fifteen, the intellectual age, the very short period of study, in which the child is rapidly initiated into the elements of useful knowledge, is no longer submitted to the necessary power of the natural laws, reflects at last, and decides in accordance with a fresh principle, the idea of utility. Lastly, — third period, — after the age of fifteen, sentiment and duty make their long-delayed appearance, "We enter upon the moral order." Abruptly, the social formation of the man comes under consideration.

Such is Rousseau's bizarre programme: thus he establishes three superposed divisions of education, three stages; and one may ask how, after this artificial distribution of the individual, the three sections of the human person can join together again, and combine to reconstitute the natural entirety formed by the body and the mind.

None the less, there is, as always, a proportion of just, true observation in Rousseau's arbitrary theory. He is right in desiring that consideration be given to the characteristics proper to each age of life, and that, for example, a child be treated, not as a man, but as a child. "Treat your pupil as his age demands. The wisest," says he, — and he evidently intends to refer to Locke, — "devote themselves to what a man should know, without considering what children are able to learn. They always seek the man in the child, without thinking of what he is before he becomes a man." And again: "Let infancy mature in the child. We have often heard of a finished man; let us at last think of a 'finished child.'"

On this point, Rousseau is not in agreement with some of our modern educators, even with those who draw their inspiration most from him. In a recent book, which is extremely interesting, *L'Éducation nouvelle*, M. Demolins, the founder of the school of les Roches, the innovator who with praiseworthy zeal is striving to acclimatize in France certain portions of the manly, free English education, M. Demolins formulates a contrary opinion. According to him, it is never too soon to treat a child as a man. "Treated as men," says he, "children actually and speedily become men." And he quotes the anecdote of a child of nine, who, very quickly indeed, — in two hours, — really became a man, simply because, having been received with his parents by an English family, the three members of this family took him seriously during his visit, and were willing to talk with him the whole time! . . .

To form men, to "manufacture" them, as it is now expressed, is the perpetual dream of educators of all times and countries. To have a certain measure of success, it is perhaps desirable to adopt a course somewhere between the two extreme opinions of M. Demolins and of Rousseau. On the one hand, it is never too early to school a child in his duty and to prepare the apprenticeship of personal responsibility by appealing to his reason and reflection, and Rousseau errs in causing the delays of which we know to this education of reason. On the other hand, however, — and here Rousseau triumphs, — it must not be forgotten that the child is a child, and that he cannot be required to exercise judgment and act as a free man when his judgment is not formed nor his liberty created. Our two pedagogues, moreover, are at bottom more in agreement than one would think. They neither wish for a premature instruction which throws the child from the beginning into abstract studies, and according to Goethe's expressions, tends to make him into "a subtle philosopher, a scholar, and not a man." M. Demolins certainly would indorse this conclusion of Rousseau's: "The ordinary education is bad because is makes old children and young professors." In the same way, as regards moral education, M. Demolins, who is especially opposed to discipline based on "the principle of authority," cannot but applaud Rousseau's exaggerations, since the latter expressly does away with all authority, and censures parents and masters who have never early enough "corrected, reprimanded, flattered, threatened, promised, instructed, reasoned."

Where it is not permissible to fall in with Rousseau's views is in the incomprehensible delay which he imposes on moral education. This is, in another manner, more pernicious than the adjournment of intellectual culture. Émile has attained his fifteenth year, and has not as yet felt any human sentiment. Whom does he love? Nobody, save perhaps his tutor, the only man whom he knows. His mind has not been opened to any of those infantile affections which prepare the social virtues. By what miracle will he suddenly learn to love mankind, after living so long in the cold, sterile isolation of a strictly individual life? Rousseau, truly, is too summary in the recital of his pedagogic methods. He says, "Émile is this; Sophie is that." He endows both of them with all kinds of marvellous qualities and virtues; but he neglects to tell us how they have been acquired. Concerning the genesis of affectionate sentiment, it is evident that he is reckoning on a miraculous result which he has done nothing to prepare. He has left Émile's heart empty for fifteen years, and in an instant he thinks that he can fill it. What a delusion! Love cannot be taught like calculation. The formation of social feeling is a delicate and difficult matter. Rousseau, moreover, complicates the problem by submitting Émile to the laws of egoism alone. As Condillac, by a series of subtle transformations, derives from primal sensation the most abstract and general notions, so does Rousseau pretend, by a strange metamorphosis, to obtain from initial egoism alone all the altruistic sentiments. Self-respect is, in his eyes, the sole and fundamental atom of sensibility. How could he forget that other atom, sympathy, which makes itself apparent from the dawn of life, and whose development cannot too soon be encouraged and stimulated? In the smile which a new-born babe directs towards the one who suckles and cares for it, there is more than the expression of a material need satisfied: there is the instinctive response of the child to the considerate tenderness of the mother. "So long as the child

ₗpays attention only to what affects his senses,
arrange for all his ideas to be limited to sensations.

'   No, on the contrary, let us open wide the
door for the sentiments, which are, indeed, only too
ready to enter. With children, it is necessary at
once to mingle mind with body.

It is known that Rousseau, in his mania for post-
ₗponement, delayed until adolescence the revelation
of religious as well as moral ideas. The reason which
he gives is that a child, with its purely emotional
imagination — and it is very likely the fault of negative education if this be the case — could only form
a superstitious idea of God, and would picture him
as a human being, an old white-bearded man, a
monarch seated on a throne. . . . Hence the pro-
priety of awaiting the age of reason before speaking
of God to Émile, so that he may straightway form a
conception of him in the ideal sublimity of his
spiritual attributes. At least, if he has deferred
to the age of eighteen the revelation of the Supreme
Being, Rousseau makes up for it by the splendor
in which he invests him. He was a deist in all
sincerity. He believed in God with as much conviction as he believed in the soul and in a future life:
"I desire too greatly that there be a God, not to
believe in him. . . ." Without seeking verification
in his other writings, the *Profession de foi du vicaire*

savoyard demonstrates it in a striking manner. It was, in his opinion, the principal portion of *Émile.* For it he would have sacrificed all the rest. It was that part of his manuscript that he intrusted to the keeping of his surest friends, fearing, in the perpetual apprehensions which the printing of the work caused him, that his enemies, and particularly the Jesuits, might cause it to disappear. This was the principal cause of the wrath and tempest of persecution which were about to be let loose against him. It was this, on the other hand, which earned him the enthusiastic praise and even the admiration of Voltaire; for it is of the *Profession de foi* that Voltaire, so hard upon *Émile,* intended to speak, when he says that this "stupid novel" contains, however, "fifty pages which deserve to be bound in morocco." At a distance, and despite a superb setting and a magnificent style, the *Profession de foi,* which is somewhat of a digression in an educational treatise, strikes us as an emphatic declamation of a vague, irresolute spiritualism. Its intrinsic value as a philosophical work is, however, of small importance. The fault we find with it is that it is the first word of religion which Rousseau made his pupil hear, if so it be that he really wishes to develop religious feeling in him. That Rousseau's conception cannot be realized is indisputable: if Émile lived, like all children, in a family and in the world, he would be a witness of exterior manifestations of religion on the part of his parents and fellow-citizens, and in his curiosity he would speedily ask what all this means: to hide God from him would be impossible. But that is not the question: what does matter, is to know whether the method employed by Rousseau responds to his intentions, whether it is of a nature to insure their success. I should think it excellent rather to produce atheists. Will not Émile, who has dispensed with God for so long, be tempted to dispense with him altogether? In his desire to communicate to his pupil the sentiment of religion with which he himself was so thoroughly imbued, Rousseau ought to have taken thought that here also a slow development is necessary, that Émile's temporary atheism is in great danger of becoming fixed, quite as much as his egoism or his intellectual inertia.

In this, as in many another particular, Rousseau has not followed his principle, which is to obey the laws of nature. Borrowing from him one of his metaphorical methods of expression, one would be tempted to imagine that "Nature," speaking, would address him nearly as follows: —

"Truly, O Rousseau, I should be very ungrateful, did I not hail you as one of the mortals who have most exerted themselves to restore my dominion.

You have avowed yourself my faithful servant. Your incense has burned on my altars. You have practised, with sincere enthusiasm, a simple, frugal life, rustic pleasures, and innocent manners, in a society given up to luxurious tastes, to vice, and the complications of worldly life. You have shown the dawn to people who used not to rise till noon. You have taken into the open air, into the broad sunshine, little children who were fading away in the vitiated atmosphere of great towns. You have protested against unnatural requirements and the caprice and artifice of fashion. You have endeavored to restore to humanity the simplicity of the primal ages. . . . All praise to you for this.

"But on how many points, believing your inspiration to come from me alone, you nevertheless have erred? I have no proof that you really understand my nature. Everybody around you speak 'of the mystery of nature's law.' Are you quite sure that you have thrown light upon this mystery and penetrated it?

"What am I in your eyes? 'The sum total, you say, of humanity's instinctive tendencies before falsified by opinion.' You forget that 'opinion' has been in part formed by me; that society is my work, that I founded it, and count for much in its organization. It seems that, in your mind, I have remained, congealing in my immobility the wild, primitive nature of the world's earliest ages. No, I am not a motionless, invariable force. I advance and keep abreast of progress. Some one who has no liking for you, but who has much wit, said humorously that you were making humanity move backwards to the barbarian epoch in which men walked on all fours and ate acorns. . . . I grant you that Voltaire exaggerates; but all the same, by vaunting the benefits of ignorance, by execrating arts and letters and all the works of civilization, have you not given excuse for this raillery?

"Heedlessly you ask that a clean sweep be made of everything that your ancestors have instituted, whereas these institutions and customs have often been dictated to them by me. You wish, in education, to take in everything the side opposed to custom, but do you not see that 'custom,' which you condemn in its entirety, could not have lasted from century to century, if it had not agreed in part with the laws over which I preside?

' I do not wish to take your errors in detail, but here is one. You rightly teach your dear Émile natural religion alone, the one religion which I can admit. You are right, acclaiming behind me Providence, my creator, to oppose the internal and profound sentiment of conscience to vain and super-

stitious forms of ritual. . . . But why, in this religious education, have you not acted in conformity
with human progress itself, which, guided by me, has
advanced from primitive superstition and the feeble
light of later theology, to the fuller light of pure
reason? Your predecessor, Fénelon, who also pleased
me greatly by the effort which he made to approach
me nearly, was wiser; and if it really is necessary
that men remain believers, he understood that the
one means of insuring their faith was to lay its
foundations early in the child's mind, by introducing
to him at first, as I have done for humanity, perceptible ideas of God, imperfect, confused notions,
whose superstitious imageries will gradually be dis-
sipated by reason, in proportion as it develops, in
order to exhibit, as far as human frailty permits,
the pure and rational conception of Him who made
me. . . .

"To sum up, O Rousseau, your great error, the
principal fault with which you will be reproached in
succeeding centuries — for I foresee the future — is
lack of belief in progress; failure to divine the great
law of the perpetual evolution of things. You have
missed my most important characteristic, which is
ceaseless motion. The word 'progress' comes
often from your pen, but you always find it evil.
It is for you, or nearly so, a synonym for decadence

and corruption. . . . Your successors, on the contrary, will consider progress as my supreme law, my essential principle, as the reason for the existence of humanity and the world. They will understand that nature is not the product of a day, that the successive acquisitions of inheritance form an integral portion of my substance.

"Let your errors be forgiven you, however, for you have loved me greatly. Others will come after you who will also think that they have defined me. They also will, perchance, be mistaken; for I am not as simple as may be thought; I am infinitely complex, and I remain the impenetrable enigma, unfathomable in its designs, whose solution will perhaps never be accomplished by man. . . ."

IV

By his visions, even those which were in contradiction with the nature whose patronage he was invoking, Rousseau has rendered signal service to the science and art of education. "His errors," said P. Girard, "are themselves wholesome warnings. By violently shaking traditionary usages, he awoke minds slumbering in routine, and by his flights of fancy he suggested and prepared just and practical solutions.

But *Émile* contains also, and in large number, general views and detailed facts concerning the various branches of education which may be accepted straightway almost without revision. These form, as it were, quite a cluster of flowers, which will blossom eternally in the garden of education. How many eloquent sayings, taken from *Émile*, do we constantly hear? How many maxims, fresh in 1762, and become almost trivial at the present time, form the current coin of our pedagogics? How many others, wrongly neglected, will be found to be of value to us?

It is now commonplace to recommend physical education. And Rousseau is not the first who, in modern times, by a reversion to the ancient mode of life, urged youth to bodily exercises. Ten years earlier, Turgot wrote, "We have especially forgotten that the formation of the body is a part of education." Rousseau, on this subject, refers his reader to Montaigne and Locke; he might also have referred him to Rabelais. None the less do we praise him for having, in his turn, insisted forcibly on precepts more frequently recommended than practised. Let us be grateful to him for entering, as he does, into minute details on clothing, length of sleep, and food, thus clearing the way for the hygienists of childhood.

Émile must strive to "combine the vigor of an athlete with the reason of a sage." He must think like a philosopher and work like a peasant. Bodily exercise is not prejudicial to the operations of the mind. The two actions should proceed in harmony. Sports were not yet fashionable in Rousseau's time, and no one can blame him, when he prophesied the French Revolution, for not having also predicted the triumph of football. He at least recommends swimming, which everybody can learn. Riding is discarded, as too expensive. When he is twenty, however, Émile will take rides, without prejudice to his long excursions on foot. Rousseau, who had walked across France, from Paris to Lyons, could not help recommending pedestrian exercise. It is, however, of the infant, principally, that Rousseau thinks. Even before it can walk, it will be taken daily into the fields and meadows, to frolic, to run about as soon as it can. Let there be no longer any question of an effeminate, confined education, suitable for making "scholars without muscle." Health and physical force are to be considered first. Rousseau comes back to this subject in his *Considérations sur le gouvernement de Pologne*. In this work he calls for the establishment in every school of a gymnasium for bodily exercise. "This is," says he, "the most important item in education, not only as regards the formation of a robust constitution, but even more on the score of morality. . . ."

Indeed, it is not solely from hygienic motives, nor for the strengthening of the body, that Rousseau proposes his scheme of education in the country, with full liberty of movement, open-air excursions, and joyous gambols: he sees in physical exercise a means of development of moral power, — a prelude to education in courage and innate virtue. Rousseau seems to be inspired by memories of Spartan life or Stoic doctrine. His Émile is rigorously brought up; he is inured to cold and heat and accustomed to privation. None of his caprices, supposing such possible in nature's pupil, are acceded to. If he is granted what he asks for, it is not on account of his having made the request, but because it is known that it is really needed. And Rousseau, who a moment ago was wisely returning from paradox to common sense, now, inversely, and with equal facility, passes from equitable, just precept to ridiculous and absurd exaggeration. Émile is to walk barefoot; he is to go about in the dark, without a candle or other light. He will, perhaps, learn in this way to have no fear of the dark, but will he not run the risk of a broken neck, "the eyes which he has at his finger-tips" seeming scarcely sufficient to insure him against a slip or a fall? Let us pass by these eccentricities in which Rousseau's genius goes astray, and let us be satisfied with proving that he anticipated all those who, nowadays, demand an active, manly education, which shall produce vigorous men, dexterous of limb and capable of standing face to face with danger; ready and able to render practical assistance both to themselves and others; truly equipped for life as regards its material occupations as well as its difficulties and moral trials.

To view Rousseau's famous theory on the necessity of serving an apprenticeship in a manual occupation from the utilitarian standpoint alone, would be to misinterpret his intentions. Undoubtedly, he saw in it a resource, an assured livelihood, should there come a time of adversity and ruin. A prescient thought for the rich man, suddenly reduced to poverty and obliged to work for his living, is not foreign to Rousseau's scheme. "We are drawing near the age of revolutions. Who can say what will then become of you?" If, however, he makes Émile a joiner, not a mock joiner, but a real workman, who attends his workshop regularly, and does not allow even the visit of his betrothed to distract him from his occupation—there are other motives governing him: he wishes to reinstate work, and more especially, manual work. "Rich or poor, whosoever does not work is a cheat." There is also the pedagogical consideration that it is not alone the head, the brain of a man, which must be exercised, as though the brain were the entire man. We should be able to use our hands as well as our reason, and because it develops physical capability, endurance, exertion, and practical acquirements, manual labor is good for everybody. Rousseau would have endorsed these recent words of M. Jules Lemaître: "Our collegians' time, wasted twice over by them, since they spend it in not learning a dead language which, if learned, would be of little use to them, might better be employed, I do not say in studying living tongues, natural science, and geography, —

that is too apparent, — but in games, gymnastics, and joinery. . . ." Especially would he be delighted to see in what honor the manual occupation to which he gave the preference is held in certain modern schools, in England, for example, at Bedale College, the prototype of M. Demolins' des Roches school, where gardening and farm work is succeeded by exercise in woodwork. The pupils are seen bringing real enthusiasm to the making of boxes, racks, and book shelves, on which they then place books bound by themselves.

The education of the sense is intimately connected with that of the body. "Not only have we arms and legs, we also have eyes and ears." In this, again, Rousseau is an excellent guide. Pestalozzi, and all the patrons of the intuitive method, all those who preach the lessons of things, are only his disciples. Everything else depends on the education of the senses. Rousseau has sometimes been compared with Descartes. He would have been the "Descartes of sensibility" following the Descartes of understanding. It is more accurate to liken him to Condillac, whom he classed "among the best reasoners and most profound metaphysicians of his time." Like the author of the *Traité des sensations*, he accepts the maxim, "Everything that enters the understanding comes through the senses." The senses are "the first faculties to form in us: the first, accordingly, to be cultivated." To this cultivation Rousseau devotes the twelve years of childhood, satisfied if, "after this long journey through the region of sensations to the boundaries of childish reason," he has succeeded in forming Émile into a sensitive being, able to see, hear, feel, calculate distance, and compare quantities and weights. . . . "Yonder is a very high cherry tree; how can we manage to gather some cherries? Will the ladder in the neighboring barn do? There is a very wide brook; will one of the planks lying in the yard be long enough to cross by? . . ."

Émile, who uses the plane adroitly later on, is clever in the use of his fingers at an early age. Rousseau, who does not say much of how he taught him to write, being ashamed, as he says, of troubling over such trifles, — and yet spelling is not taught by nature, — takes great interest in the study of drawing: "Children, who are great imitators, all try to draw." In these attempts, however, it is not the art of drawing for its own sake which Rousseau values so highly, it is more on account of the profit accruing from it to the training of the senses and the organs of the body. Practice in drawing makes the eye more accurate and the hand more flexible. The child, of course, is only to draw from nature he is not to imitate imitations; objects will be his only models.   Let us add that all idea of beauty is absent from this first initiation into the material representation of things.   Rousseau is not thinking of producing an artist; the result will, at most, be a geometrician; moreover, if he recommends drawing, it is less for Émile to imitate objects than to become acquainted with them.

Sensations prepare ideas.   By perceiving objects clearly, Émile trains himself to judge, that is to say, to grasp their affinities.   His first judgments, however, are confined strictly to the domain of tangible knowledge.   He must obtain his instruction from actual objects and not from words.   "Do not talk to the child of matters which it cannot understand. Use no descriptions, no eloquence, no figurative language.   Be satisfied with introducing him to objects opportunely.   Let us transform our sensations into ideas, but without leaping at one bound from perceptible to intellectual objects. — Turgot had already said: 'I wish abstract and general notions to come to children in the same way that they come to men, — by degrees, and by a regular progress from sensible ideas.' — Let us pass slowly from one sensible idea to another.   In general, never replace a thing by its representation unless it be impossible to show the thing itself.   I dislike explanations and discourses. Things? things? I cannot repeat often enough that we attach too much importance to words; our chattering education produces nothing but chatterers. . . ."

A time comes, however, when the employment of words and abstract ideas is forced upon us, when something more than perceptible objects must be studied. In the selection of studies which he offers Émile, Rousseau is obedient to a principle, a single criterion, — that of utility. This great visionary is a utilitarian. His programme certainly is short: it is calculated to displease those who demand a complete education, universal knowledge for a youth. But in his practical tendencies he inaugurates, with omissions, the programmes of realistic instruction which will be adopted more and more for fresh generations. Rousseau may well be the father of this instruction which our contemporaries are endeavoring, not without gropings, to establish and organize under the fine title of up-to-date education. The name is found: the thing itself is by no means realized.

However this may be, the end in view is now settled. A fact which must be recognized is that intellectual education should be a direct preparation for life, and that the current system is in part bad and doomed to disappear, because, between the

ultra-speculative studies which it inflicts on youth
and the realities of existence, between the scholar's
life and the man's calling, there is a profound disa-
greement,—what Taine called an "incompatibility."
Goethe was even then saying, fifty years later than
Rousseau, however: "So much theoretical knowledge, so much science, is what exhausts our young
people, both physically and morally. They lack
the physical and moral energy necessary to make
a suitable entry into the world. . . ."

Rousseau's language is to the same effect. It has
been seen that he wished to endow Émile with physical energy. He was no less thoughtful for moral
energy. This philosopher, thought to be lost in the
land of chimera, says: "When I see that, at the most
active time of life, youths are kept to purely specu-
lative studies, and are afterwards, without the least
experience, cast upon the world and into business,
it seems to me the offence against society is as great
as that against nature; it does not, therefore, surprise
me that so few people know how to order their conduct. What bizarre deception causes the persistent
teaching of so many useless things, whilst the 'art
of action' counts for nothing? Nominally, we are
formed for society, and we are instructed as though
each of us had to pass his life in a cell, engaged in
solitary thought."

"The art of action," is not this the watchword of future education? To Rousseau belongs the credit of having uttered it, though he may not have had the talent necessary to combine the means which can make it effective. There is some temptation to reply to him that it is not by rearing Émile in solitude, "as though he had to pass his life in solitary thought" in the fields, that a youth is made fit for actual human life. But what does one more inconsistency matter? Rousseau, at least, understood that instruction must be relieved of all the superfluity of show study. He, however, carries this also to excess. How can we refrain from reproving him for the way in which he despises the old classical studies, the ancient languages in particular, which he dares to describe as "a useless feature of education." As an educator he went too far in rejecting the literary sources, by draughts from which, as a thinker and writer, he formed his genius. Men of letters will protest, and not unreasonably, against such culpable infidelity; but all men of good sense will praise him for having shown that the aim of education is not the accumulation of sterile knowledge in the memory; that it is the formation of intelligence by a discreet introduction to a moderate selection of useful studies, giving preference to attainments which nourish the mind and train it to be ready for action, rather than to those attainments which are only a useless ornament.

Émile has reached the age of fifteen: his short studies have come to an end. He has little knowledge, but he is prepared for knowledge of every kind, and this is the most important consideration. Do not take him for a scholar: he is not meant to be one; but he has a taste for knowledge. His natural curiosity has been aroused. According to the saying which Rousseau borrows from Montaigne, if not taught, he is at least "teachable." No prejudice has perverted his mind or impaired the accuracy of his judgment. He knows nothing on authority; he has acquired all his knowledge for himself. He has not been taught the facts themselves, so much as the method of finding them out. He has been told to look, and he has found. Thus will he continue all his life on the path to knowledge, which he has been shown, "long, stupendous, tedious to follow."

In Rousseau's methods of instruction we perceive two excellent tendencies: firstly, that, in order to thoroughly master what is learned, a personal effort is required, a research, a sort of original discovery, and not merely an effort of memory and mechanical acquisition; secondly, that the most important thing is not the knowledge acquired at the end of study, the light baggage of attainments which serve too often as an excuse for mental slumber after leaving college, but the desire to enlarge one's knowledge and aptitude for acquiring it. Those who draw up the overladen, encyclopædic programmes of our education, before beginning deliberations which almost always result in yet another burden, even when schemes of reduction are the order of the day, should read over and meditate well upon this pleasing passage from *Émile:* "When I see a man carried away by his love for knowledge, hastening from one alluring study to another, without knowing where to stop, I think I see a child gathering shells upon the seashore. At first he loads himself with them; then, tempted by others, he throws these away and gathers more. At last, weighed down by so many, he ends by throwing all away, and returning empty-handed. . . ." Is not this a very clever and correct picture of many modern scholars, weighed down by their burden of useless acquirements, embarrassed with ideas of every kind, disgusted by wearisome studies, and finally leaving college almost empty-handed? Rousseau attaches himself here to the great tradition of French pedagogics, a tradition too often set at naught in our schemes for study. It advocates, as Nicole said, "the use of knowledge only as an instrument for the formation of reason"; which, of course, applies to knowledge only in so far as it plays a part in that general culture aimed at by secondary education.

If we now examine in detail the programme of utilitarian studies which Rousseau intends for Émile, we shall be surprised more than once, both on account of what he includes and what he omits. Rousseau is the most disconcerting and deceptive of educators. Thus, he forbids the study of history, and this is one of his most provoking paradoxes. In this he is, however, logical with himself. Since Émile is "to be removed from humankind," he must be denied knowledge of the dead as well as contact with the living. History is the great agent by which social consciousness is developed; now, in his early education, Émile is only an individualist, a perfect egoist, without any social sentiment. It is known, moreover, what special argument Rousseau advanced and upheld to excuse the omission of history; namely, that a child is incapable of understanding it. History is as much out of his reach as the philosophic idea of God: as though there were not a history for children, a history made up of description, narrative, and great men's lives. Fortunately, in the matter of history, as in so many other things, Rousseau contradicted himself, and to rectify his errors or correct his semi-voluntary paradoxes, it is sufficient to appeal from Rousseau to Rousseau. As legislator of the Polish government, his language is quite different from that used by the theorist of *Émile*. Far from condemning history, he will be found rather to carry it to excess.

In language which, in its animation, recalls the words used by Rabelais to extol the study of natural science when he makes Gargantua say to his son: "I want you to be acquainted with the fish of every sea, river, and spring, — with all the birds of the air, the trees and shrubs of the forest, and all the herbs of the earth; . . ." similarly, Rousseau says: "I want the young Pole, when learning to read, to read things concerning his country; so that when he is ten years old he shall be acquainted with all its products; when twelve, all its provinces, roads, and towns; when fifteen, its entire history; when sixteen, all its laws; thus, every fine deed which has been done, and every noted man who shall have lived, in all Poland, shall fill his heart and mind." The education of a little citizen, a future patriot, could not have a better preparation. Let us take note, however, that Rousseau's retraction is not complete; he speaks only of national history, leaving the general history of mankind, which has no interest for him, a sealed book to his pupil.

Émile, having been cheated of knowledge of the

ethical world, will, in compensation, be nourished with knowledge of the material world. The study of nature must come before everything else. Is not the same thing thought at the present day by the educators of the United States, who attach so much importance to knowledge of natural truths? What does cause surprise, is that, in his programme, Rousseau should put astronomy in the forefront. Auguste Comte also mentions it first in his catalogue of sciences and in his system of positive education. One has the right to ask why. Utility cannot be its recommendation. Émile is to travel, but he is not intended to navigate, and it does not seem at all likely that he would find a knowledge of the constellations and heavenly bodies of any use to him. Likely enough what decided Rousseau was the fact that astronomy, physical astronomy at least, is one of the sciences most suitable for the application of his beloved method, — the method of conscious and direct observation of things. Émile, who does not know what a class room or a study is, gains his knowledge in the open; he contemplates nature's great spectacles, and reflects in the presence of the starry sky.

In virtue of the same system, astronomy is followed by physical science and geography, keeping to tangible and concrete studies in which abstraction plays the least important part. Émile learns geography without maps, during his walks and in presence of the actual objects. "Why all these representations? . . . I recollect seeing somewhere a text-book on geography which began thus: 'What is the world? — A pasteboard globe.' . . ." The only method of preventing these fallacies is to introduce to the child the thing itself and not its artificial representation.

An elementary knowledge of astronomy, physics, and geography will be practically everything till the age of fifteen is reached. Has Émile learned grammar? Not otherwise than by using his mother-tongue and hearing his master talk: "Always speak correctly in his presence." At all events, at this age, he as yet knows nothing of either ancient or modern literature. Poets and prose-writers of every degree are as unknown to him as historians. Rousseau, before Condorcet and so many others, is already an expert in scientific education; but in science itself he rejects all that is pure speculation and abstract generality. He admits that there is a chain of general truths by which all sciences are linked to common principles and successively unfolded. But "with this we have nothing to do" in the formation of the mind. "There is another, altogether different, which shows each object as the cause of another, and always points out the one following. This order, which by a perpetual curiosity keeps alive the attention demanded by all, is the one followed by most men, and of all others necessary with children." Thus, in the study of physics, arrangements will be made to connect all experiments by a kind of deduction, so that, assisted by this connection, children can arrange them methodically in their minds, and recall them when required. All this, however, only deals with the establishment of a material order between perceptible truths. To the senses, Rousseau subordinates even the deduction of ideas and their linking together. No doubt it is on this account that mathematics do not figure in Rousseau's programme. Émile, who is forbidden to read even La Fontaine's *Fables*, on the ground that he would not understand them, does not seem to be any more acquainted with arithmetical rules. . . . Decidedly his instruction is insufficient and limited. Rousseau had none of that holy horror of ignorance which characterizes later educators: "Ignorance," said he, "never did harm; error alone is pernicious." Education has an importance beyond instruction. "We prefer good men to scholars."

Rousseau is more happily inspired in the education of the will than he is when dealing with the mind. Despite appearances, and despite the continual presence of a guardian whose surveillance would not seem altogether favorable to the development of individuality, Émile is really brought up in liberty. It is certain, and we do not forget it, that Rousseau was chiefly deficient in character and energy. He could never overcome temptation. "It was always impossible for me to act against my inclination." All through his life he was the plaything of circumstances, the victim of his passions. This, however, rather disposed him to desire for Émile a better education than the one from which he himself suffered, an education of a kind to accustom a child to act on his own initiative, in fine, an education of "self-government": "The child must be left to himself, both as regards body and mind. The boon of freedom is worth many scars."

By emancipating the child, Rousseau intends, primarily, to make him happy, and that at once; for the poor little one may die young, and before he dies he must taste life. Now a child's happiness, like a man's, consists in the exercise of liberty. Rousseau had a sincere affection for children. In all his wise recommendations concerning the care to be taken with an infant, an inspiration of tenderness almost unknown before his time may be detected, a lively feeling of pity for these frail creatures who are, as a first consideration, to be made to live. What a number of tender things he has written on children! What treasures of affection left unused by this culpable father! "Nature made children to be loved and succored. . . . Does it not seem as though a child displays such a sweet face and affecting manner only that everything which comes near it may be touched by its feebleness and may hasten to its assistance?" Tutors of all ages will have to draw inspiration from cautions like the following: "If you do not open your heart, others' hearts will remain closed to you. It is your care and affection that you must give."

But beyond the child's present, and the joy in life which he wishes to insure for it immediately, Rousseau also thought of the future, and the requirements of social life. By the independence which he grants it from the cradle, when he abolishes the imprisonment of swaddling clothes; as later, in boyhood's years, when he wars against prohibitions and verbal injunctions, in order to substitute for them instruction from facts alone and the living lessons of example,—"Example, example! lacking this, success with children was never obtained;"— when, finally, he appeals to all that is spontaneous in the intelligence and personal in the will of his pupil, it is evident that he wishes, in this way, to form men of stronger physique, more vigorous morals, and greater control over their actions, than the scholars of old-style colleges, in the austerity of their cloistered life, were prepared to become, and than the students of our modern high schools are, even at the present day, in spite of the achievement of so much progress.

Note, however, that Émile's education is by no means one of complacency and enervating laxity: rather is he submitted to a regimen of severity. His room is in every way like a peasant's. And if Rousseau has made a gleam of joy shine in his life by the liberty which he grants him, he none the less wishes the child to know how to bear suffering. Suffering will leave Émile stronger, and is the first thing that he must learn. Primarily, he is thus early armed against the evils which existence has in store for him. But he also learns to sympathize with the misfortunes of others.

Man is an apprentice, with affliction for his master.

Earlier than De Musset, Rousseau said in his fine prose, "The man who is ignorant of affliction, knows neither human tenderness nor the sweetness of commiseration."

In spite of the sort of antisocial sequestration

which Rousseau imposed on Émile for fifteen years, it must not be imagined that he gave up all idea of making a feeling, loving being of him a little later. Even as a child, he must be shown "this world's unfortunates." The spirit of fraternity fills Rousseau's generous soul to overflowing: "Proclaim yourself aloud the protector of the unhappy. Be just, humane, and kindly. Do not give alms alone, give charity." Rousseau advances toward modern socialism. Note, for example, this bold reflection: "When poor people were willing there should be rich people, the rich promised to take care of those without means of subsistence, either from their property or labor." Arrived at man's estate, Émile spends a part of his time in doing good to those around him. When in love, he does not allow the thought of Sophie alone to absorb him. He interrupts his attentions to his betrothed that he may act as a true philanthropist. He travels the country; he examines the land, its productions, and their cultivation; he himself ploughs on occasion. His knowledge of natural history is utilized for the benefit of the cultivators; he teaches them better methods. He visits the peasants in their homes; and, after inquiring into their needs, he helps them with his person and his money. Does a peasant fall ill? He has him cared for; he himself attends

to him. Simple medicine, indeed, and such as can,
be allowed by an enemy of doctors, consisting, as it
does, in more substantial nourishment. He makes
his future wife a partner in these good works: he
takes her to visit the poor, to see a laborer who
has broken his leg, and whose wife is about to be
confined. "With her gentle, light hand," Sophie
puts dressings on the wounded man: she waits on,
pities, and consoles him.

By birth and extraction Rousseau was of the
people. He remained one of them by the simplicity
of his tastes, living like a laborer, fond of associat-
ing with the lowly, though at times he did not
disdain the complaisance of great lords, and was not
insensible to the caresses of great ladies. Does this
imply that in his educational projects he worked
directly for the people and for the people's instruction? No. Émile, if not a gentleman like Locke's
pupil, is at any rate of the middle classes, rich and
well born. But by the fact that he eliminated ancient
languages and all expensive studies, and replaced
"book" education by the simple, natural cultivation
of the talents which every human creature brings
into the world at its birth, Rousseau suggested
the idea of the universal emancipation of intelligence; he inspired the democratic idea of making
instruction general. He did not wish for the "cere-

monious" education of the rich, for what he still called "exclusive" education, which only tends to distinguish from the common people those who have received it. Moreover, the object being to make men, and not scholars, the poor would, in truth, "require no education." Freed by their life of toil from all the conventions of society, subjected to nature's laws alone, "the poor can of themselves become men."

Rousseau — and for it he has been severely blamed — wished to form, not a man of a certain station, or of a settled profession, but just a man. He thought too much, says Taine, of "man in the abstract," and not enough of actual man, such as he is made by the circumstances of time and place, and as he should be trained by education, so that he may be fitted for his place in life. "Whether my pupil be intended for the army, the church, or the bar, matters little to me. Before he adopts the vocation of his parents, nature calls upon him to be a man. How to live is the business I wish to teach him. On leaving my hands, he will not, I admit, be a magistrate, a soldier, or a priest: first of all he will be a man. All that a man should be, he can be." Let us give praise to Rousseau for having reminded men, that they have a personal destiny, that first and foremost they should, if pos-

sible, set up and strengthen in themselves the principles of human dignity. Let us, however, censure
him for keeping too strictly to the absolute, without
considering the contingencies and relative conditions
which require the individual to graft on the common
stem that branch of special acquirements which the
place that he will occupy in life exacts, as a condition of being worthily held. He did not sufficiently reflect on the principle, which is becoming
more and more insistent on recognition, that education must be diversified and specialized in a score
of forms, that it may be in conformity with the
various exigencies of social labor, no less than in
correspondence with the multiplicity of individual
talents. Rousseau has erred in a manner analogous
to those religious educators who, forgetful of the
present life, and thoughtful only for the life to
come, — which alone has any value in their eyes,—
aspire only to the rearing of a pure and virtuous
creature for the bliss of life everlasting. The
philosopher of nature and ideal humanity joins
hands, without suspecting it, with the mystical
constructors of God's City. When his "one and
indivisible" education is finished, Émile may be the
type of a man; but he must not be expected to be
an engineer, a doctor, or a lawyer. Of what use,
then, will he be in society, since he can bring no

special attainments beyond those proper to his trade of joiner?

It is well that Émile has learned a manual trade; it is well that he is "fit for all stations of life"; but perhaps no harm would ensue from the addition of a professional preparation for one of the functions to which society calls men.

At times, however, the practical spirit awakens in Rousseau and timidly takes its revenge. After he has betrothed Émile to Sophie, he forces him to leave her and travel abroad for two years. By a fresh contradiction, Rousseau, who so long kept Émile from coming into contact with his own compatriots, and did not introduce him into society till he was twenty, now enlarges the circle of his social connections to the extent of wishing him to enter into relations with the men of other countries. Travel, says he, forms part of education: travel, not for pleasure, however, but for instruction and study, a kind of "scholastic course" abroad. Émile must be acquainted with the genius and ways of foreign nations; truly it was wasted time to forbid so long the reading of histories! It is true that books are worth nothing. It is with his eyes that Émile should see foreign things, as all other things. Rousseau never abandons the method of direct observation. If we are to believe him, the French are, of all the peoples of the world, the greatest travellers. Was this true in 1762? We doubt it. At all events, it is regrettable that it is not now the case. Émile travels, then. So that, in the course of his wanderings, he be not turned aside and diverted from the serious objects of his observations, Rousseau has taken care that he is enamoured before his departure. The love sworn to Sophie is to preserve him from all dissipation, and to shelter him from passion and vice in the great towns which he visits. On his travels, Émile devotes himself entirely to his observations, which are not, however, concerned with monuments and antiquities, or on the relics and ruins of the past. That is of no interest; it is the present which should be known. Émile is not an archæologist. His attention is directed especially to questions of government, to customs and laws. He will study politics and comparative legislation on the spot. And when he returns to his native land, he can usefully examine the institutions of France, in order to judge of them by comparison. Perhaps he may deem them inferior and bad, and will consequently be moved to the ambition of contributing to their reformation. On the contrary, this cosmopolitan of a few months' standing may have become a more ardent patriot, attached to his own country the more for being better informed regarding the vices and evils of other countries. Let us be assured, if Rousseau had lived in our time, he would have joined his eloquent rebukes to those of the present-day educators, who urge young Frenchmen to become colonists. It was not a fit time to think of that in 1762, when, through the fault of its monarchy, France was on the point of losing her magnificent colonial empire.

The most important of the results of Émile's travel is that he learned "two or three foreign languages." Rousseau did not give him much time for that; difficulty of achievement, as we know, does not trouble him. It is scarcely apparent how Émile, who as yet has studied no foreign language, living or dead, is able so rapidly to learn German and English. What matters this? The main thing is that here again Rousseau pointed out the goal and drew attention to the importance of studying the living languages. Further, in the course of his travels, Émile took care to cultivate acquaintance with foreigners of parts, so that, having returned home, he continues to correspond with them. This exchange of letters, which lasts his whole life, will raise his thoughts and sentiments above national prejudice, and will make him a citizen of the world. Thus did Rousseau prepare the way for the modern educators, who protest against Frenchmen confining themselves to devout contemplation of themselves, and who exhort them to mix with the universal life of humanity, that they may see and comprehend the world outside.

V

Émile is a perfect man; to be worthy of becoming his wife, Sophie should be an ideal woman. But Rousseau is far from successful in this second part of his task; and woman's education, as displayed by him, is certainly not so well understood as man's.

It is with special care, however, that Rousseau wrote the fifth book of *Émile*, which is almost entirely devoted to feminine instruction. He composed it, he says, "in a continual ecstasy" (he was at the time the guest of the duchess of Luxembourg, at Montmorency), "in the midst of woods and streams and choirs of birds of every kind, with the fragrance of the orange-blossom in the air"; and he in part attributes "the rather fresh coloring" of these pages, more poetical than philosophical, to the pleasant impressions which he experienced in this earthly paradise. But he lived there with his Thérèse, — a companion and model ill-fitted to assist him in the conception of an educated woman. He was constantly at the mansion and received visits from brilliant and titled ladies, — a companionship ill-suited perhaps to the conception of a simple, strong woman, whose likeness he wished to sketch.   The material surroundings themselves, also the delicious abode at Mont-Louis was more conducive to revery than analysis.   The book of *Sophie* is only a pleasant idyl.   The poet and novelist decidedly gain the upper hand in it.   Of all things that Rousseau fails to understand, said Saint-Marc Girardin, it is woman that he understands least.   Certain of her refinements, her noble dignity and pure moral grandeur have, at all events, eluded him.   He has for her more tenderness and loving adoration than true respect and esteem.   Even in the most exquisite descriptions of his heroine, looked at both physically and morally, an indefinable, sensual appetite is always to be detected, — a memory of common or worldly women, coquettish and artificial, whom he had known and loved.

Sophie, moreover, is not altogether an imaginary being.   When outlining her lineaments, Rousseau asserts that he had in his mind an actual model. Sophie existed then, and the name alone was of his invention.   Dead in the springtime of her life, he merely "revived" her to make "this lovable girl" Émile's companion.   The story is dramatic and touching.   Having read *Telemachus*, at the age of twenty the real Sophie was smitten with love for

Fénelon's hero, and, being unable to find in the world a youth like him, she died of unsatisfied love, of languor and despair. Fénelon is thus responsible for the death of a maiden. . . . How does it come about that this tragic episode of real life did not prevent Rousseau from making his Sophie, who was the image of the other, too sensitive and romantic? It is true that, overtaken with tardy remorse, he seems to have realized the vanity of his efforts, and himself emphasized the insufficiency and inefficacy of his scheme of feminine education, when, with strange irony, in the *Roman des Solitaires*, he shows us the virtuous Sophie become an unfaithful wife, although she saw in woman's misconduct nothing but "misery, disorder, unhappiness, opprobrium, and ignominy."

Between Émile's education and that which Sophie receives, there is more than a contrast, there is an abyss. Rousseau emancipated Émile; he enslaves Sophie. To the same degree that he showed himself bold in his views on the "foundation" of men, is he timid, backward, and conservative in his ideas on woman's education. The apostle of individualism renounces his doctrine. He subordinates woman to man; of her he makes an humble subject whose only value lies in ministering to her husband's happiness. He confines her strictly to her duties as

daughter, wife, and mother. If he invites her elo-
quently to fulfil her obligations as a teacher, he forgets to provide her, by a sufficiently well-developed
instruction, with the means of acquitting herself
worthily in this great mission. Finally, he does not
appear to suppose that woman also has a claim to
acquire personalty, that she legitimately aspires to
extension of her acquirements and development of
her faculties, so that, with her enlightened intelligence and emancipated reason, she may truly be
man's equal and, indeed, the "abstract woman."

Rousseau's maxim is that woman should be obedient to man, that her existence is, as it were, con-
ditional on that of man. Listen to these continual
repetitions which, like a monotonous refrain, re-
appear on every page: "The whole education of
women ought to be relative to men. . . . Woman
is specially made to please men, to be useful to
them, to make themselves loved and honored by
them, to rear them when young, to care for them
when grown up, to advise them, to console them, to
render their lives agreeable and sweet to them, —
these are the duties of women at all times, and should
be taught to them from their childhood. . . . All
their caprices must be overcome so as to make them
submissive to the will of others. . . . Dependence
is the woman's natural condition. . . . Woman is

'created to be all her life subject to man and to man's judgment. . . . It is a law of nature that woman shall obey man. . . . She is created to give way to man, and to suffer even his injustice. . . ."

There is, then, no idea of educating Sophie for herself. Rousseau does not, at heart, admit the equality of the sexes. He says of woman that she is "an imperfect man," that in many respects she is only "a grown-up child." I am aware that Rousseau, with his customary inconsistency, contradicts himself in other passages: "The question of superiority," he says, "must not be urged: differences account for all. . . . Each sex has qualities suited to its destiny and part in life. . . . It is perhaps one of the marvels of nature that two beings so similar, and at the same time so differently constituted, should have been made. . . ." But he insists upon these differences: "It is demonstrated that man and woman are not constituted alike, either in temperament or character." By speaking of differences, does not one singularly compromise the idea of equality?

What, then, is Rousseau's idea of the character and temperament proper to woman? He expounds it to us twice: first, somewhat ponderously in the long pages of general philosophy which begin the fifth book of *Émile,* and form a kind of outline of feminine psychology; and later, with a quite poetic charm, when, putting away abstract considerations, he raises the curtain to show Sophie in her grace and beauty.

Woman is weak. She is passionate: "If she pretends to be unable to bear the lightest burdens, it is not only to appear delicate, it is to arrange excuses for herself and the right to be feeble should occasion require." Her heart feeds on unlimited desires of love; it is true that "the Supreme Being added modesty" in order to counterbalance and restrain them. Sophie, like all women, is a natural coquette. She is fond of finery, almost from the moment of her birth. She is not displeased to display "her well-turned leg." She is inquisitive, too much so. She is artful, and necessarily so, to compensate for what she lacks in strength. "You tell me that little Sophie is very artful," wrote Rousseau to the prince of Würtemberg, "so much the better! . . ." Artfulness is a natural talent, and everything natural is "good and right." The instinct of artfulness, then, must be cultivated. Rousseau, however, is good enough to admit that it is as well "to prevent its abuse." Sophie is talkative. She is imperious. She is by nature a glutton — here Rousseau forgets that he has declared all primitive instincts to be excellent. Does not the doctrine of original goodness apply to woman with as much force as to man? Sophie is temperate, but she has become so. . . .

So much for the defects, and we have minimized them. The portrait is not overdrawn. Let us now examine the other side: the good, the qualities. Woman is more docile than man. She has more delicacy than man. She is more skilful in reading the human heart. Her dominant passion is virtue. Let us note, moreover, that it is never certain whether Rousseau means to speak of woman in general, or of the exceptional creature which he has personified in Sophie. Her chief happiness is to make her parents happy. She is chaste and honest till her last sigh: here the ideal woman is obviously intended, the one of whom he says, "A virtuous woman is almost the equal of the angels! . . ."

But woman, in general, is not man's equal. A charming being whom Rousseau idolizes, yet none the less binds down to the subordinate position of her part as younger sister, and inferior in the human family. Her natural qualities must be respected, be they good or ill. It does not seem as though Rousseau wishes even her faults to be corrected, because they may perchance help her to captivate men. A woman should remain a woman. It would

be folly to wish for the cultivation of man's qualities
in her. Rousseau, who, on so many other points
forestalled the tendencies and innovations of the
modern mind, can in no wise be considered an expert
in what is nowadays called "woman's rights."
Nothing would have offended him more than the
claim to mingle and assimilate the two sexes in
the same habits and functions. The modelling of
woman's education and life on man's would, to him,
have seemed an aberration, a usurpation of the
rights of the stronger sex, and, in another sense, a
profanation.

It is more especially when he considers woman's
intellectual faculties that Rousseau shows himself
unjust to them. He admits that their judgment is
earlier formed, but he asserts that they soon allow
themselves to be outdistanced. They have not
sufficient attention and accuracy of mind to succeed
in the exact sciences :— we may note, in passing, that
Émile gives no evidence of any training in them,
either. — Everything that tends to generalize ideas
is outside their competence. All their reflections
should centre in the study of men, or in agreeable
acquirements which have "taste" as their object.
Search after abstract truths is not suitable for them.
No women philosophers or women mathematicians
then: Rousseau would have refused another Sophie

—Sophie Germain — the right to exist. Works of genius are beyond them. Is it not true, however, that, as a novelist, George Sand, to mention no others, has indeed some genius, at any rate as much as Rousseau? . . . In short, feminine studies should relate exclusively to practical matters, and Rousseau would willingly repeat Molière's words:—

Is it not seemly, and for many reasons,
That a woman should study and know so many things. . . .

Sophie's instruction, then, is extremely limited. It could not be otherwise in a system which, on the one hand, lowers the function of woman, and, on the other hand, disparages her intelligence and powers. How can she be asked to acquire knowledge which will be useless to her in her rôle of humble subordination, or to undertake studies which exceed the capacity of her mind? In her library, Rousseau puts only two books, *Telemachus* — and even this is out of place, if it be true, as Rousseau tells us, that it excites a girl's imagination — and *Comptes faits*, by Barrême. Sophie ought to understand thoroughly the keeping of household accounts. She must be a true housewife, knowing the prices of provisions, superintending her servants, such a wife as Xenophon had already pictured the partner of Ischomachus.

In her youth, Sophie was especially engaged in learning needlework: she sews and embroiders.

The wife of Émile, who has his working hours, must not be capable of neglecting manual occupations. Rousseau felt the importance of what is nowadays called the "household education." Sophie cuts out and makes her own dresses. She has a preference, it is true, for lace. Why is this? It is because there is no form of needlework which "gives a more pleasing pose." Sophie remains somewhat coquettish, even in her household occupations. Rousseau wishes — must he be blamed for it? — a woman to be always attractive and elegant, to do everything gracefully. Nothing should detract from the charm of her personal appearance, even when she is cooking. Somewhat "foppish," Sophie prefers burning the dinner to soiling her cuff. Is Émile, who dines badly that evening, consoled by admiring the spotless cleanliness of Sophie's attire? There is, let us confess, something sickly and too delicately refined in the education of this young woman who, for example, dislikes gardening, giving as a reason that "the earth seems dirty to her."

Sophie cultivates accomplishments, less for her personal benefit than to contribute later to her husband's amusement. She has a nice voice, and sings; a taste for music, and plays. She can dance. But from all other points of view, she is decidedly an ignoramus. A little arithmetic — enough to total

up the household expenses — has been taught her:
"Perhaps women should before all learn to cipher,"
according to the natural method, however: "A
little girl can easily be persuaded to learn arithmetic, if care be taken to give her cherries for her
lunch only on condition that she count them."
But literature, poetry, and history she knows nothing of. Bluestockings are an affliction. "Every
learned girl will remain single all her life, when only
men of sense are to be found." Rousseau would
certainly not have approved of the creation of high
schools, nor even elementary schools, for girls.
"There are no colleges for women: what a misfor-
tune. . . . Would to God there were none for
boys. . . ."

However insufficient Émile's instruction may
seem to us, Sophie's remains on a yet much lower
plane. She is in no wise the enlightened woman
whose action is necessary to regenerate the family
and society. Rousseau, though he detested Paris,
has made of her a frivolous Parisian, who is rather
a grace than a power in the house, a charming plaything or a thing of fashion.

It is not alone by her insufficient instruction,
which practically amounts to nothing, that Sophie
differs from Émile; it is also in the nature of her
education. The system on which a woman is

educated should be different from that adopted in the case of a man. Émile does not make his entry into society till he is about twenty; Sophie is admitted at a very early age. Before becoming a wife and mother, she must be acquainted with society and life. Reversing the usual practice by which a girl is kept in almost cloistered seclusion, and a woman is thrown into the whirlpool of society life, Rousseau wishes Sophie to go often to balls, plays, suppers, accompanied by her mother, of course; but once married, she shuts herself up in the peace of domestic life. Here we have quite a fresh inspiration, a scheme of education in the English or American style. If Sophie is shown society, it is, however, that she may be made to feel its emptiness and vice, and may be sickened of it forever. Is it quite certain that this precocious emancipation would give the results that Rousseau expects? Let us praise him, nevertheless, for having introduced the elements of gayety, good temper, and liberty, into a girl's life. Sophie is merry and "skittish"; she is not to live "like a grandmother."

Another difference: from the earliest years of her infancy, religion will be mentioned to Sophie. The reason which Rousseau gives for this is the very one which we advanced against him, when he delayed for Émile this religious teaching which he hastens for Sophie. If we had to wait until a woman was able to conceive a true idea of religion, "to discuss these deep questions methodically, we should run a risk of never mentioning it to her." This is, then, only a fresh proof of the little esteem which Rousseau professed for feminine intelligence. Submissive to the judgment of others, Sophie blindly accepts her mother's religion. "Every girl ought to have the religion of her mother, and every wife that of her husband." Opinion and authority, so boldly expelled from Émile's education, resume their sovereign sway when Sophie is in question. "Opinion," says Rousseau, emphatically "is with men the tomb of virtue, with women it is its throne": which is to say that, in their beliefs as in their behavior, women are subject to the opinion of others. Women's religion, moreover, is confined "in the narrow circle of dogmas which derive from morality." She is simple and reasonable, — "reasonable" is a word already used by Mme. de Maintenon. "Persuade her well that no knowledge is useful except such as teaches us well-doing. Do not make theologians and logicians of your daughters: teach them such of heaven's things alone as are of use for human wisdom. . . ." Morality is the essential part of religion, and we serve God by good actions.

At times Rousseau hesitates, desisting from keeping woman in her state of subordination; he seems to perceive that, to be a wife and mother, Sophie needs a little more instruction. "There are," says he, "only two classes in humanity: those who think and those who do not think." And guiding Émile in the choice of a wife, he exhorts him to put aside all consideration of fortune or social rank, "to take for his wife even the hangman's daughter, so little should he care for class." What does matter, is that a wife should think, know how to bring up her children, and be able to live in communion of ideas with her husband. In that case, however, is it not evident that it would be indispensable to arrange for her a wider and more thorough instruction? "It is the husband," replies Rousseau, "who will teach her everything and be her instructor. . . ." I admit that he will complete and widen her instruction, but on condition that, already as a girl, she has been initiated into the things of the mind. Let her be forbidden to read novels, — "never did a chaste girl read a novel," — this is already very severe; but how sanction her never having a serious book in her hands and being as ignorant of literature as of science, "fatal science"? This is, nevertheless, really the conclusion come to by Rousseau, who seemed to fear that by instructing woman she might be made man's equal, and that "the preeminence which nature gives to the husband might thus be conveyed to the wife."

It is true that Rousseau, if he abases woman on the one hand, exalts her on the other. "Women," says he, "have a supernatural talent for governing men. . . ." But this so-called supernatural talent is nothing but their grace and beauty, and, in short, the very natural power which they exercise over man's senses. "The best households," he says again, "are those in which the wife has most authority." Yes; but in his theories, this authority is not that of a cultured intelligence and tested reason; it is simply a rule founded on gentleness, made lasting by the little methods which a wife's ingenuity or indulgence suggest to her. It it by her caresses that Sophie orders, it is by tears that she threatens. Mme. Roland's father, discussing the choice of a husband with her one day, said to her, "I understand you would like to subjugate some one who thinks himself the master, doing everything that you wish. . . ." Sophie is of the same school. She appears to obey, but in fact she reigns and governs, and her sovereignty is due only to the seductions of her sex.

A strange book, it must be admitted, is this romance of Sophie's education. In it charming things are mingled with pedantic dissertations.

Delicate thoughts are near neighbors to declamations that might be described as the ramblings of a disordered brain. In it the highest lessons of virtue alternate with loose passages of vicious gallantry, and with rather free observations. The eulogy of Spartan or Roman manners is followed by pages in which one guesses that Rousseau found as much pleasure in reading Brantôme as in reading the Bible, — which he had read right through more than six times, during the sleeplessness of his nights of sickness. We must not require from Rousseau the lofty purity of sentiment which the mission of woman's educator demands. How can we be touched by his enthusiasm for decency, modesty, and seemliness, when we have just heard him say that, "Sophie does not display her charms; on the contrary, she covers them up, but in covering them up she knows how to suggest them"? Or again, "In Sophie's simple and modest attire, everything seems to have been put in its place only to be removed piece by piece. . . ." We do not know, sometimes, when reading *Émile*, whether we are in presence of a severe moralist or a man of gallant adventures. What is not subject to doubt, is that the too realistic memory of Mme. de Warens, or the ideal representation of Mme. Sophie d'Houdetot, — whom he loved too much "to wish to possess her," — accompany and partly direct Rousseau's pen when he is sketching Sophie's portrait. . . .

Do not let us, however, finish with this unfavorable impression. If Sophie is not the strong, sensible, and enlightened woman that we could wish her to be, if she is rather a "weak, silly woman," more graceful than reasonable, seeking, above all, to please, not disdaining, in her coquetry, to display her white hand and shapely foot, let us, nevertheless, salute in her a pleasant wife, who can retain her husband's affections, a devoted mother, who feeds and brings up her children; lastly, one who compensates by rare merits for the imperfections of her incomplete education. Of her independent life and her own personality, Rousseau takes no heed. It is conjugal intimacy alone which can make of two beings united for life one moral person. Woman is, then, only a part, a fragment of this moral person. As a compensation she will be the most seductive of companions for the man whose complement she is. Sophie is not one of "those who banish from marriage everything that can be agreeable to men." She is not a wearisome devotee, enslaved by those rigorous dogmas which, "by pushing duties to absurd limits, make them impracticable and vain." Rousseau asserts that in his time "so much had been done to prevent wives from being amiable, that husbands had been made indifferent." To the scolding, sullen wife he opposes one who is smiling and cheerful, who wishes to please and succeeds in doing so; who makes the obligation of fidelity pleasant and easy for her life's companion. One may be tempted to wonder how, after all the evil that he spoke of women, Rousseau met among them so many impassioned admirers. It is because, if he did not assign to them their true rank, he at least flattered them; he encouraged them in their tendency to rule by the power of their natural charms alone. He liked and cajoled them a great deal. Observe with what satisfaction he forgets himself when depicting the early love passages between Émile and Sophie, what delicious trifles occupy him in the portrait which he paints of his heroine. To figure her as perfect, he draws upon all the races of humanity. Sophie has the temperament of an Italian, the pride of a Spaniard, and the sensibility of an Englishwoman. All that she lacks to be perfect is, perhaps, the good sense and sedate simplicity of an instructed and cultured Frenchwoman. She also is a pupil of nature: "She makes use only of scent which comes from flowers." — "I never praise her so much as when she is simply clothed. . . ." There are wise and beautiful sayings in the confusion of the fifth book of *Émile;* as, for example: "Show woman in her duties the very source of her pleasures and foundation of her rights. Is it so difficult to love so as to be loved, to make oneself amiable so as to be happy, to make oneself esteemed so as to be obeyed, and to respect oneself so as to be respected? . . ." Many other passages explain, without however justifying it entirely, the opinion of a German educational historian, Frédéric Dittes, who went so far as to say that he considered the fifth part of *Émile* to be "the best book which has been written on woman's education." And, at all events, Sophie, despite the gaps in her education, is already the modern woman, created not for the church and the convent, but for family life; despite her defects, she possesses this precious and fresh quality, that her virtue is amiable.

VI

THE influence of Rousseau and his pedagogic thought was preponderant, as we shall see presently, chiefly in Germany. But the fame of *Émile* was universal, and the echoes of it have not yet died away. As a man who sought after glory, and whose gloomy temper took umbrage at everything, Rousseau complained that *Émile* did not obtain the same success as his other writings. He was truly hard to please! . . . The anger of some, the ardent sympathy of others; on the one hand, parliamentary decrees condemning the book and issuing a warrant for the author's arrest, the thunders of the church and the famous mandate of the archbishop of Paris; on the other hand, the applause of philosophers, of Clairaut, Duclos, and d'Alembert, . . . what more, then, did he want? *Émile* was burned at Paris and Geneva; but it was read with passion; it was twice translated in London, an honor which no French work had received up till then. In truth, never did a book make more noise and thrust itself so much on the attention of men. By its defects, no less than by its qualities, by the inspired and prophetic character of its style, as well as by the paradoxical audacity of its ideas, *Émile* swayed opinion and stirred up the most generous parts of the human soul. It were too difficult to enumerate all the imitations and counterfeits which have been prompted by Rousseau's powerful influence, to say nothing of the refutations, contradictions, and criticisms. The end of the eighteenth century witnessed the appearance of quite a succession, a posterity of Émiles: first, *Anti-Émiles*, then *Christian Émiles*, *Corrected Émiles*, *New Émiles*, Émiles retouched, improved, shortened, amplified, and even Émiles converted to social life. In many a place were attempts made to put into practice the education extolled by Rousseau; children were brought up in the Jean-Jacques style. Fashion took part in it. There were also "dresses in the Jean-Jacques style," of which it was said, in peculiar language, that they were "analogous to that author's principles."

Rousseau had already carried utopianism very far; it was, however, carried still farther. Let us mention, for example, a very curious book, which is, as it were, a caricature of *Émile*, *L'Élève de la nature*, by Gaspard de Beaurieu. However silly this utopianism may have been, it passed through no less than eight editions, between 1763 and 1794. So as the better to insure his Émile's isolation, de Beaurieu had the idea of shutting him up in a wooden cage till he reached the age of fifteen; then he landed him on a desert island. . . . Nothing more extravagant could be conceived. And yet Rousseau did not disclaim his fantastic disciple: he loved his paradoxes to the extent of excusing and approving their exaggeration. In a letter of the 25th of May, 1764, he wrote: "I have read *L'Élève de la nature.* One cannot think with more intelligence, or write more pleasantly. . . ." Without confusion, Rousseau looked at himself in the magnifying mirror in which an indiscreet admirer had already exaggerated his dreams. It is true that he added, not without a touch of irony: "I advise M. de Beaurieu to always keep more to subjects which can be dealt with by descriptions and representations, than to those needing discussion and analysis. . . . An agricultural treatise would suit him perfectly. . . ."

Happily, Rousseau found more serious imitators. The end would never be reached if we mentioned all the great men who, in literature or politics, make for him in posterity a long train of admirers. How many revolutionists fed on the maxims of *Contrat social,* and felt the political influence of Rousseau, a "disastrous" influence, however, according to Auguste Comte, who describes his doctrines as "anarchical"? Are not Chateaubriand, George Sand, and many others, the progeny of the author of *La Nouvelle Héloïse?* . . . But we have only to occupy ourselves in this place with educators, and it is perhaps on them that the salutary action of Rousseau's thought has most usefully been exercised.

The revolution of 1789 did not last long enough to make it possible that anything of permanence in the matter of education should be accomplished. But Rousseau's inspiration is apparent in the majority of the projects which it improvised without ever succeeding in putting them into operation. The chimerical plans of Saint-Just and Lepelletier de Saint-Fargeau' emanate directly from *Émile.* In year III, Marie-Joseph Chénier asked "that the method pursued by Rousseau in Émile's education should be applied to the entire nation."

Rousseau's teachings, in truth, obtained more theoretical admiration than practical application. It has never been proposed, for example, to bring into existence those *Schools of the fatherland* imagined by the gentle and sentimental Bernardin de Saint-Pierre, the cheerful utopian, idyllic reformer, and nature enthusiast. At least it must be admitted that in suppressing punishments and rewards in his educational scheme, in removing the motive of emulation, and on yet many other points, Bernardin merely copies Rousseau, whose friend, confidant, and consoler he had been.

Women have had a special fondness for Rousseau. Who loved and extolled him more than Mme. Roland, "Jean-Jacques' daughter," or the "Jean-Jacques of women," as she has been called? In 1777, she wrote to one of her friends: "I love Rousseau beyond expression. . . . I carry Rousseau in my heart. . . ." She especially esteemed him for having revealed to her domestic happiness and the ineffable delights which may be tasted in family life. For her part, Mme. de Staël greets *Émile* as "an admirable book, which puts envy to shame after exciting it," and she tells us that, in her youth, she fell in love with negative education. Rousseau's influence is perceptible on even those women educators who most contested the conclusions of *Émile*. The principal work of Mme. de Genlis, *Adèle et Théodore*, often recalls *Émile et Sophie:* the indirect lessons, the artificial and prepared scenes, dear to Rousseau, are found again in it. Mme. Necker de Saussure, though opposed to the principles of eighteenth-century philosophy, often draws inspiration from him, after contradicting him. Like him, she sees in the child a being apart, whose education has rules of its own. She holds again, after him, the idea of a progressive development of the faculties, and consequently that of the sequence of methods appropriate to the age and powers of the child.

It has been said of Rousseau that he introduced into French literature the genius of the north, that he was of a German or English temperament. I do not know whether this view is very accurate. Rousseau knew nothing of Germany. He did not like the English. "I have no penchant for England. . . ." He was brought especially under French influence during his wanderings across France and his long sojourn in Paris; and, indeed, nourished by classical reading, he may quite as properly be regarded as a representative of the extreme sensibility of southern races. What, however, is certain, is that this child of Geneva, if not of "Teutonic" genius, became Teutonic by his influence. As the lamented Joseph Texte has shown in his fine book, *Jean-Jacques Rousseau et les origines du cosmopolitisme littéraire*, his light has gone forth into all lands. The success of his works and the propagation of his ideas made him a cosmopolitan.

There is hardly a German writer but has borne him favorable testimony, usually, indeed, enthusiastic homage. Basedow, a pedagogue who had in his time a great but little deserved reputation, swears only by Rousseau, whose theories he uses, in his way, with frenzied zeal. Having no son, he

finds consolation in calling his daughter "Émilie."
Lavater shows himself as eager as Basedow for the
reformation of education in the direction of the
doctrines of *Émile*.   But here are weightier authori-
ties.   Lessing declares that he cannot pronounce
the name of Rousseau "without respect."   Schiller
extols "the new Socrates, who of Christians wished
to make men."   Goethe calles *Émile* "the teacher's
gospel."   Kant affirms that no book "moved him
so deeply."   He read it with such avidity, that, in
his strictly ordered life, "the regularity of his daily
walks was for a time disturbed."   In his little
Treatise on Pedagogics, many principles are bor-
rowed from *Émile:* for him also nature is good.
Herder, who has been named "the German Rousseau," cries out, "Come, Rousseau, be thou my
guide"; and in a letter to his beloved Caroline, he
acclaims *Émile* as "a divine work."   In his *Levana*,
Jean-Paul Richter says that, of all previous works
to which he feels himself indebted, it is to *Émile*
that he must assign the front rank, that "no preceding work can be compared to it."   But it is to
Pestalozzi especially that is due the honor of
developing and popularizing, whilst attempting to
apply them, the methods of Rousseau, whose works
had early fixed his imagination: "The system of
liberty founded ideally by the author of *Émile*

excited in me a boundless enthusiasm." Lastly, Froebel, who wished to replace books by things, who had nothing so much at heart as the preservation of the child's spontaneity, deserves a place in the golden book of Rousseau's disciples. And it is not only in the great men of Germany that Rousseau inspired new sentiments: thinkers of lesser importance, Jacobi, Heinse, Klinger, and yet many others, took part in this adoring veneration which Germany professed for the French educator.

Rousseau has been somewhat less appreciated in England. There also, however, despite the scandal of his ridiculous rupture with Hume, he found immediate favor and success. *Émile* was translated in London as soon as it appeared; and a second edition was soon called for. In 1789 David Williams said, "Rousseau is in full possession of the public attention." It is true that opinion was occupied with the political theories of *Contrat social* rather than the pedagogical conceptions of *Émile*. Somewhat neglected for a century, Rousseau was again brought forward by Mr. John Morley, and also by a distinguished educational historian, Robert Quick. The latter opines that "the truths contained in *Émile* will survive the fantastic forms in which the author enveloped them." In his eyes, *Émile* is "the most influential book ever written on education." This is also the opinion of John Morley, who states that *Émile* is "one of the seminal books in the history of literature." Again we have George Eliot's avowal: "Rousseau has breathed life into my soul, and awakened new faculties in me. . . ." And lastly, is it not true that Rousseau's principle, the return to nature, dominates the pedogogics of Herbert Spencer, the most brilliant educational theorist of contemporary England?

Apparently it is in America that Rousseau has met with least sympathy, and we must not be much surprised at this. How could this dreamer, this indolent idler, this heroic representative of the sensibility of the Latin races, be gifted with the power of pleasing the virile, rugged minds and busy, practical temperaments of the citizens of the New World? In the study which he recently devoted to him, Mr. Thomas Davidson admits his discomfiture. On examination, the most vaunted theories of Rousseau have disappointed him. He did not find in them the firm and solid substance which he expected to obtain from a study of *Émile*. And yet, when closely examined, American education, as we see it practically developing at the present time, has more than one point of resemblance with the ideal pedagogics of Rousseau. One of the leaders of American education, Dr. Charles W. Eliot, the revered president of Harvard University, summarizing the progress accomplished in his country during the nineteenth century, draws attention especially to the introduction of two essential things into the school curriculum: nature study and manual training. The American child is no longer a logical phantom, stuffed with words and abstractions, but a living creature, working with hands as well as mind. . . . But is not all this Rousseau? Similarly, Dr. Eliot points out that an improvement has come about in discipline. In religion, love has been substituted for fear; in politics, people have begun to understand that the government of nations should no longer remain what for thousands of years it has been, — the work of an absolute and arbitrary will; that in its place must be put the free government of the people by the people; and consequently people have come to think that the modern and more accurate conception of a good government for a nation's citizens held lessons for us on the subject of a good government for children, who also should be freed, as far as possible, from the yoke of the old tutelage, and trained in self-government. . . . But is not this also Rousseau?

Without our suspecting it, Rousseau's pedagogical spirit has insinuated itself into and penetrated the methods of teaching and the educational practices which the present time endeavors more and more to honor. Go into one of the infant schools: object-lessons are given; the children are shown the things themselves, and the method of observation and direct intuition is put into practice. Make obeisance: Rousseau it is who inspired these methods. . . . Pay a visit to one of those English colleges which M. Demolins is attempting to imitate and popularize in France: there you will find masters who are both guardians and professors, never leaving their pupils, who, like them, live in the college from morning till night; how can we avoid recognizing in them the actual descendants of the imaginary tutor to whom Rousseau confided the care of Émile? . . . Enter one of those American schools in which the abuse of books and manuals is condemned, and in which the mental slavery of mechanical instruction has been exchanged for methods of intellectual freedom, so that the child shall acquire what it is requisite to know as far as possible by himself and by his personal effort. In this, again, you will be forced to acknowledge the hand of Rousseau. . . . Wheresoever discipline has become more liberal, where active methods are supreme, and where the child is kept constantly in a state of interest, lively curiosity, and sustained attention, his dignity being at the same time respected, there we may say Rousseau has passed by.

Utopias perish, but the truth endures. The spirit survives the letter. We cannot, indeed, hope to derive from Rousseau's pedagogics a definite and final system of methods and procedure. But what is perhaps better, he handed on to his successors and still imparts to all who read him a spark, at least, of the flame which burned in him. As Mme. de Staël said, he has perhaps discovered nothing, but he has set everything ablaze. His eloquence was the most powerful appeal ever addressed to parents and masters to exhort them to take their task as educators seriously. With him, education became a sacred mission, a sublime ministry. Into educational questions he instilled a spirit of life, a movement of passion, unknown to the cold, dry pedagogues who had dealt with such questions before him. Henceforth the educator's part is raised and ennobled; and, by the fire of his enthusiasm, Rousseau stamped the science and art of rearing men with the majesty and solemnity of a kind of religious revelation.

And as, in Rousseau's works, time, eliminating his mistakes, maintains and develops the living seed which he sowed abundantly in the field of education, so with the man himself, in his character and acts, distance and the flight of ages hide from us defects and misdeeds, which, little by little, return to shadow, in order to let us see only his qualities and virtues.

If Rousseau still exercises great seduction over the human intellect, it is not solely by virtue of the force of his innovating genius. Neither is it by the mere effect of his style, sometimes somewhat heavy, but whence at every moment flashes forth the lightning; that style which earned him the title of the "king among prose-writers." It is because, behind the writer and thinker, we feel the pulsations of the most sincere heart which ever throbbed in the breast of man. Voltaire's enmity must have been strong indeed to blind him to such a degree that he could write: "It is useless for Rousseau to play now the stoic and now the cynic: he belies himself continually. The man is factitious from head to foot." The opposite is the truth. Rousseau's great charm, the secret of the irresistible sympathy which he inspires, is precisely that he yields his entire self, that he displays himself, as it were, stripped to the skin. With a soul more sensitive than meditative, a mind more æsthetic than philosophic, he did not know that self-possession, that mastery of a firm, cool judgment, which permits a thinker to control the turmoil of sentiments and the confusion of images, so as to construct and organize a system of connected and consistent argument. From this arises the hesitations and contradictions of his thought. On the other hand, a dreamer guided by his senses, he could offer no resistance to instinctive impulses; whence the failings of his moral life, failings, moreover, which we are aware of only through his own confession. Many men of genius have doubtless had these same passions and frailties; they, however, have hidden them as much as possible, whilst he spread them abroad in the shameless candor of his *Confessions*.

There is nothing fixed or precise in Rousseau's moral philosophy. Rules of conduct strongly enough established to suffice for the rearing of men cannot be found in it. There is something of the stoic in him, but the epicurean gets the upper hand. "The man who has lived most," says he, "is not the one who counts most years, but the one who has most felt life." To enjoy life, that is the object he prescribes for Émile. It is true that Rousseau immediately writes: "Shall I add that his object is also to do good, when he is able? No; for that is itself to enjoy life. . . ." The accomplishment of duty is presented, not as a law and an obligation, but as a source of pleasure. The stoic reappears when Rousseau advises the limitation of desires, when he says that the essentially good man is he who has least needs, who is self-sufficing. In this respect, Rousseau generally acted in accordance with his maxims. He was intemperate at times. In his youth he pilfered from M. de Mably's cellars bottles of a white wine for which he had a liking, and many other peccadillos could be mentioned. But taking his life as a whole, he was sober, simple in his tastes, an enemy of luxury, temperate, and even austere.

What he lacked, more than lofty and noble inspirations, was the necessary energy to keep to them. His senses and imagination governed his existence. Could it be otherwise, considering the education which he had received? While yet a child, his father read novels with him till morning; and only when he heard the swallow's notes did he say, "Let us go to bed, Jean-Jacques! . . ." A friend of virtue rather than virtuous, agitated rather than active, a slave to his sensations when he would fain have been the apostle of liberty, tossed about by the caprices of his fancy when he claimed to be establishing among men the reign of sovereign reason, capable of being at times a hero of courage and disinterestedness, to descend afterwards to unworthy and even criminal actions; sentimentalist and idealist, yet often allowing I know not what coarse echo of erotic sensuality to be heard in his most poetic hymns to love and beauty, in the torrent of his life he mingled muddy waters with the purest streams. At times intoxicated with sublime thoughts, he nevertheless evaded the strictest and pleasantest duties; and he has not absolved himself from his faults by a too platonic enthusiasm for righteousness. Too often has he lived selfishly, seeking the solitude which was soothing to his reveries, flying the men who troubled his pride. He was imbued with his own opinion to the point of willingly parting company with common sense, and was so elated with his personality that he thought himself an exceptional being, of a race apart: "Why did Providence cause me to be born among men, having made me of a species different from them? . . ."

Yet this somewhat wild misanthrope has contributed to a greater love of life by introducing into it more liberty, joy, and faith; by arousing and strengthening, according to Mme. Roland's phrase, "all the affections which attach us to existence": devotion to humanity, enthusiasm for the ideal, friendship and love. He has been generous and helpful. His dream was the happiness of man: "Make your paradise upon earth, whilst awaiting the other." He worked for a fresh, rejuvenated society, freed from the prejudices of the past: "Woe to thee, O thou stream of custom!" In an age of courtiers, he courageously safeguarded his right of free speech, and under an oppressive rule he maintained his independence at the cost of his happiness.

He was a citizen. One of Geneva's sons, he drew from the traditions of his first fatherland the love of liberty, the republican pride: "With us, maxims are imbibed with the mother's milk." In a society of sceptics and profligates, he was simple and a believer. Literary critics have praised Rousseau for introducing into France the dreamy melancholy of northern lands. Yes, but this melancholy is not found in *Émile*, which is, on the contrary, an optimistic book, with a joyous confidence in the future. Really living and fertile minds are those which look, not to the past, but to the future ages: Rousseau is of their number. In his sovereign disdain of antiquated tradition, he prepared the youth of the newly dawning era. With Voltaire, said Goethe, a world has come to an end; with Rousseau, a world begins. The eighteenth century, especially with Rousseau, is the rally to eternal nature, the commencement of a forward movement, a bold anticipation of the future.

I am willing that Rousseau be criticised and his errors blamed: but let us not be forbidden to admire him. He will not cease to be read, followed, and obeyed, in some, at least, of his prescriptions. He will always be a leaven of life and moral regeneration. He can proudly say to his critic, "Strike, but listen." Above all, he will be loved to all eternity.

I am well aware that Mme. du Deffand, who reproached him with wishing to plunge everything
back into chaos, called him "an antipathetic
sophist." But this is merely an exception, a voice
lost in the chorus of praise which is everywhere
uplifted in his honor. The women at all times have
been enraptured with Rousseau, and men have been
no more niggardly with the tribute of their devotion.
"I love *Émile*," said Saint-Marc Girardin, and he
learnedly expounded his reasons. He is not the
only one who has spoken in this way. "It will
always be impossible for us not to love Jean-Jacques
Rousseau," declared Sainte-Beuve fifty years ago.
And recently, the same declaration came, like a
refrain, from the pen of M. Jules Lemaître: "It is
impossible for me not to love him: I feel that he was
good." Let us love him, because he was indeed
good, because, thanks to him, a breath of humanity
and good-will penetrated and softened men's hearts,
because he himself loved truth, and because he conceived an ardent love of justice, and from his childhood was inspired with transports of anger at its
violation. Let us love him and pity him also because
of his sufferings. Let us leave to curious and prying
minds the task of deciding what was the cause of
these sufferings, the mental malady, the kind of
madness with which he was afflicted. We wish

not to know whether he were neurotic, hysterical, or simply melancholy mad. What is certain and enough for us, is that he was a man of heart and of genius to boot.

BIBLIOGRAPHY

OF Rousseau's own works, besides *Émile*, should be read:—

Projet pour l'éducation de M. de Sainte-Marie (1740).
La Nouvelle Héloïse, 5th part, Letter III (1761).
Émile et Sophie ou les Solitaires (1778).
Lettre à Christophe de Beaumont, archevêque de Paris (1763).
Considérations sur le gouvernement de Pologne et sur la réforme projetée en 1772 (1772).

In the *Correspondance*, the Letters to the prince of Würtemberg (1763), and *passim*.

Only the most important and recent of the numerous publications dealing with *Émile* and Rousseau's ideas are mentioned below:—

F. BROCKERDOFF, *J.-J. Rousseau, sein Leben und seine Werke,* 3 vols., Leipzig, 1863.

H. BEAUDOUIN, *La vie et les œuvres de J.-J. Rousseau,* 2 vols., Paris, 1871.

SAINT-MARC GIRARDIN, *J.-J. Rousseau, sa vie et ses ouvrages,* 2 vols., Paris, 1875.

J.-J. Rousseau jugé par les Genevois d'aujourd'hui, lectures given at Geneva, on the occasion of the centenary of 2d July, 1878, Geneva, 1879. See especially: *Les idées de Rousseau sur l'éducation,* by ANDRÉ OLTRAMARE, and *Caractéristique générale de Rousseau,* by H. FRÉDÉRIC AMIEL.

JOHN MORLEY, *Rousseau,* 2 vols., London, 1888 (1st edition, 1873).

E. RITTER, *La famille et la jeunesse de J.-J. Rousseau,* Paris, 1896.

Streckeisen-Moulton, *J.-J. Rousseau, ses amis et ses ennemis*, 2 vols., Paris, 1865.

A. Chuquet, *J.-J. Rousseau*, in the *Great French Writers* series, Paris, 1893.

Davidson, *Rousseau and Education according to Nature*, in *The Great Educators series*, New York and London, 1898.

J. Texte, *J.-J. Rousseau et les origines du cosmopolitisme littéraire*, Paris, 1895.

A. Espinas, *Le système de J.-J. Rousseau*, in *la Revue internationale de l'enseignement*, vols. XXX and XXXI, 1895 and 1896. See also: Musset-Pathay, *Histoire de la vie et des ouvrages de J.-J. Rousseau* (1821); Robert H. Quick, *Essays on educational reformers*, London, 1868; Rousseau's *Émile*, translated and abridged by E. Worthington, with notes by Jules Steeg, Boston and London, 1883; *Émile*, abridged and annotated by William H. Payne, New York, 1893; Hanus, *Rousseau and Education according to Nature*, New York, 1897; M. Gréard, *L'éducation des femmes par les femmes;* and finally, articles or chapters devoted to Rousseau by M. Brunetière, *Études critiques sur la littérature française*, 3d and 4th series; by M. Faguet, XVIII° siècle: *Études littéraires*, 1890; by Taine, *Les origines de la France contemporaine: l'Ancien régime*, 1882; by Melchior de Vogüé, *Histoire et Poésie*, 1898; by M. E. Lintilhac, *Littérature française*, etc.

www.ingramcontent.com/pod-product-compliance
Lightning Source LLC
LaVergne TN
LVHW011018200726
843509LV00011B/1145